FEBRUARY, 1945

CHAPTER ONE

THE lights were switched off in Central Hall during daylight hours and on that afternoon in late February, 1945, the dimness gave Charles the immediate impression of being a ghost in his own past. He had just come in through the side, staff door that was the only entrance to the old, abandoned, main foyer. There, in the shadows of the great locked main doors and high, wide, bricked-in front windows, he stopped to look around, leaning more heavily than usual upon a single walking stick that was all he now needed and that he had left on an ante-room couch before going in to his Medical Board this morning. ' . . . see you again in eight weeks, Captain Bradley . . . enjoy your sick leave . . . mightn't be a bad idea to use some of it getting your tropical kit in good order. . . . '

When he had last used that side door it had been late January, 1941, and by then Central Hall had been unlit in daylight to save electricity for four months, and the long ground floor corridor that ran across its open far end had been permanently artificially lighted. But from where he stood the corridor lights were shaded by the elegant curve of the marble, carpetless, front stairs rising to the open, wrought-iron balustraded and once semi-circular first floor landing. Before he had left in 1941, the entire right side of the Hall and first floor landing had been blocked by a new wooden wall. Charred, soaking remnants of red carpet were stripped from the stairs. The stone pedestals that still lined the left wall had lost their busts of long-gone physicians and surgeons which, in varying stages of demolition, had been removed in sacks from the floor. The huge notice, now faded and begrimed, had been nailed to the exterior of the locked main doors: NO ENTRY. WILL ALL PATIENTS AND VISITORS TO ST MARTHA'S HOSPITAL PLEASE ENTER THROUGH CASUALTY.

Charles looked up at the wooden wall with the bemused expression of a mature man hearing a distant echo of his youth. Both at the time and in retrospect, the fifty-seven consecutive nights of the first London blitz had seemed to him too similar for individual identification, with one exception. He remembered more clearly one particular night in the second week of September, 1940. On that night he had been twenty-three and a junior house-physician on-duty in Casualty, when a high explosive bomb had sliced through the roof between Casualty and Central Hall, exploded in the main dispensary that lay between them, and sparked off every cylinder in the main oxygen store directly under the dispensary. He had never known which of the violent blast waves had blown his then fourteen-stone figure through one of Casualty's sandbagged windows and flattened him, breathless, bruised, but otherwise unharmed, on the stone flags of Casualty Yard. He recalled vividly how, lying gasping like a stranded fish and though half-blinded by smoke and dust, he had seen the sheet of flame shooting through and high above the roof and transforming to pale fingers the cones of the powerful searchlights raking the roaring, smoking, blackish-red sky, and how he'd thought, if this hellish din doesn't lay-off I'll go crackers.

He grimaced self-derisively. Who didn't, first time round, he thought. Took a bit of time to catch on that either you managed to switch-off, or cracked, period. Unless, of course, you were switched-off, period.

Now he was back on his first return to London since leaving Martha's for the Army. Four years' active service had accustomed him to war ruins, and containing his emotions. What he had just seen on both sides of the Thames and of the outside of his parent hospital had slightly raised his fair eyebrows and tightened his long firm mouth that, though still good-humoured in repose, was less sensitive than when he had left. He had noted, almost academically, that only three of the hospital's original eight blocks remained standing, only one of the four former Sisters' and Nurses' Homes and that all around the three blocks, sticking up like teeth in a gaping mouth, were mounds of rubble, flattened gaps of filled-in craters, and two blackened, roofless shells it had taken him a few seconds to identify as Block 2 (Maternity), and Block 6 (Theatre).

The surviving Nurses' Home and its neighbour, the Doctors' House, faced the hospital across the wide main road running parallel with it for over half a mile. From what Charles − and their occupants − regarded as the luck of the draw, all the buildings lining the opposite side of the road were, relatively, intact. Missing roof tiles, cracked chimneys, ceilings, walls, and occasional boarded windows had become as natural to London's wartime life as National Identity cards, ration books, clothing coupons and general shortages and went as unnoticed by the occupants across the road as the sandbag and blast walls guarding all the hospital's usable entrances and bricked-in ground and first floor windows. All its blocks had been built in widely spaced parallel lines to face the road and back onto its long, wide terrace that overlooked the southern embankment, and with riverside balconies from the first floor upward. By January, 1941, all the upper floors had been emptied and now, in the three blocks, the glassless windows gaped from empty, dusty, useless wards. In those first weeks of 1941 every salvageable item had been removed to an assortment of old Army wooden and nissen huts that from then had housed the main body of the great voluntary hospital, its Nurses' Training and Medical Schools and was named,

9

officially, St Martha's-in-the-country, and unofficially, first 'Martha's Hut', and after, the Hut.

Charles had lifted his eyebrows in a different way at the vast notices festooning ruined and intact walls and the terrace's stone balustrade that he had first glimpsed when his taxi crossed Westminster Bridge. Those notices read: ST MARTHA'S HOSPITAL, LONDON. DOWN BUT NOT OUT. OPEN TO ALL PATIENTS. And on the roadside by every gateless entrance – the gates having gone in one of the 1940 scrap metal collections – other, smaller notices above padlocked wooden collecting boxes: PLEASE HELP OUR RE-BUILDING FUND.

'London started its own re-building fund, driver?'

The elderly man who had just pulled up his taxi outside the Doctors' House eased up the peak of his old tweed cap. 'Not saying one wouldn't come in handy, sir. But no sense doing more than make-do-and-mend till you're sure what you bungs up new won't come down sharpish.'

Charles glanced up at the large, grey, long-cabled barrage balloons poised all over the sky. 'I thought the flying bombs had stopped.'

'Seems like this month, sir. Not heard the one doodle-bug all February, I haven't. But if he's short on his doodles, he's not short on his rockets – least, not as you'd notice.'

'Sorry. Forgotten the V2s. Many coming?'

'Tidy few.' He nodded at the walking stick. 'Been in hospital out in the country?'

'Near York.'

'And when d'you last get London leave sir?'

'First go from early '41.'

'Ah, well.' The driver's tone and shrug were resigned. 'Bound to be a mite out of touch, sir. Never been much in the papers nor wireless on the rockets, same as there wasn't much on the doodlebugs. Stands to reason. No sense letting Jerry know when he's got hisself another bull's eye, is there, sir?'

'None.' He looked at the ruined hospital. 'Martha's had a rocket?'

The old man smiled grimly. 'If she'd copped the one, sir, you'd not have to ask. Only take the one to finish off old Martha. Only takes the one to finish off whatever it gets, so what I says is, why worry? Different in the old blitzes – different with the doodlebugs – hear all that lot coming, see, so get deep enough and get your head down and you got a chance. Not like that for rockets. If one's got your number on it, you got no chance no matter how deep you go. Can't hear the rockets coming, see – can't see 'em coming, and nothing the RAF, the ack-ack nor the balloons can do to stop 'em once they're coming. Like I says, if Jerry's chalked on your number when he pushed his little button you got no more worries, so why worry?' He eased his cap peak a fraction higher. 'Mark you, sir, if what the papers and wireless say is kosher, shouldn't be too long before the lads are over the Rhine – and I'll not say they're not taking their time getting there – still, once they got their feet dry I don't reckon it'll be long before Jerry's asking for his cards. Then all we got to do is finish off the Japs and that's our lot – and not before time. I reckoned the four years I went for a soldier last do was long enough. Come September, be six from this kick-off. So you've got in four years' time sir? Where'd you get the Blighty one?'

'Italy.'

The driver nodded to himself. He had spotted that this long streak of a bloke had had his time in the sun when he flagged him down. His shrewd glance now encompassed the faded purple Royal Army Medical Corps beret, the faded Military Cross and 8th Army ribbons on the obviously new battledress, the entwined snake medical insignia in the blouse lapels and the signs of recent illness lying over the fading yellowish-tanned, taut, square-jawed face. A bloke as knew how many beans made five, mused the driver, and for all the stick and for looking a mite peaky

11

and being a non-com (non-combatant), not a bloke he would have fancied running into on a dark night in no man's land if he was Jerry. 'That left leg doing nicely, sir?'

'Fine, thanks.' He offered a ten shilling note. 'That's all right.'

'Thank you, sir! Much obliged. Enjoy your leave. All the best.'

'Thanks. Same to you.' Charles picked up his grip and greatcoat to leave them temporarily in the Doctors' House with the hall porter – who was to prove an elderly portress – as the chimes of Big Ben striking two floated over the river.

'Dear me, two already. You should be off, Nurse Thane, and you, Dr Brown, at lunch.' Sister Alexandra smiled placidly upon the small, dark-haired girl in a fourth-year student nurse's uniform and staff nurse belt standing facing her across the desk and the black-haired medical registrar sitting on her right, writing notes. 'I'm sorry to eat into your off-duty, Nurse Thane, but I'll be most grateful if you would nip up for the blood as Nurse Martin and I are alone until Nurse Burton gets back from her lecture at three.'

'It'll only eat up a few minutes, Sister. Should be there by now. I rang the In-Patients' Lab. again whilst you were at lunch and they said they'd been promised it before two and if it didn't come they'd create blue murder and let us know.' Nurse Thane's voice was as soft and pleasing as her general appearance which, even in her ultra-starched uniform, gave the impression that her small trim, figure was boneless. That she was not strictly pretty was seldom noticed, as her expressive, near-violet eyes were beautiful. She glanced at the electric clock on the wall above the open ward doorway. 'Must've come, Sister. If not, I'll join in the creating.'

Dr Brown glanced sideways at her retreating back and

12

the clock without interrupting his writing. 'Who's having the haemorrhage, Sister?'

'Our fridge, doctor. The In-Patients' Lab.'s been too short of Group O all morning to spare any for ward reserves. Our poor fridge has only two pints in hand.'

'Could top it up with plasma.'

'Whole bloods suits it better.' She eyed him maternally. He was twenty-seven, and she was only one year older, but four years ago at the Hut he had been the new cardiac houseman when her then fiancé had been in his second year as cardiac registrar. 'Suits me better,' she confided. 'I get a bit edgy when we've only two Os in reserve.'

Dr Brown looked up smiling and thrusting back the long black forelock that slanted over his high forehead. 'I don't buy that one, Mrs Ames. You're so well-balanced you're downright unbalanced. What news of the gallant Major?'

'All well, last letter, thanks.' Both tapped the desk. 'Jolly glad to be finally shot of Antwerp, but naturally a bit browned off at being constantly short of supplies, though luckily not morphine and penicillin.'

'Where in hell would any of us be without those two? And how in hell we coped before penicillin burst upon us last summer still gives me the shakes.' He reached for the much-used single sheet of blotting-paper. 'Presumably, it's having run too far ahead of their supply lines that's been holding up the chaps. This my lot for now, Sister?'

'Yes, thanks.' She didn't comment on his other remarks, as, whenever possible, she avoided discussing – but not reflecting upon – disturbing subjects. 'Lunch, for you.'

Dr Brown glanced again at the clock. The shortest route from Alexandra Ward to the In-Patients' Pathological Laboratory was via the ground corridor and front stairs. The communal staff dining-room lay off that corridor at some distance beyond Central Hall. If he timed it right he would meet Sarah Thane returning with the blood, which was an unexpected break he didn't intend wasting. He wanted her to pull a personal string for him and in his considerable experience of such matters the best results were achieved when the request was unexpected, apparently unpremeditated, but carefully rehearsed.

'Not to panic, Sister.' He sat back looking at her sweetly chubby, serene face and then around the long wide ward that was 'Alex' to staff and patients. His own face was thin, narrow, dark-eyed, lively with intelligence and humour and just missed being good-looking. 'If any of us chaps show up in the dining-room before lunch is over on paper – spreads alarm and despondency.' He took another look up and down the ward. There were sixteen beds backed against each long side, and two against the far end walls on either side of the hardbound-battened, once glass-panelled doors that opened onto the terrace. Alex was on the ground floor of Block 3, and, like all five above ground wards, a 'combined' ward. In normal wartime circumstances, the left side was medical, the right surgical and, at present, only the first two medical beds and the first seventeen surgical were occupied. 'All female, the dining-room staff, Sister. Risk giving the lot their coronaries and the backroom boys that keep the books and our erudite Senior Medical and Surgical Officers'll go clean round the bend.'

'I expect they would, Doctor,' Mrs Ames agreed with the placidity no one in Martha's, London, had yet seen ruffled even though her transfer from the country and promotion to Sister Alex in early June last year had coincided with the first onslaughts of the flying bombs that for weeks had overwhelmed Alex, the hospital and all London's general hospitals with civilian casualties. The inrush had fallen to a steady trickle in mid-September when the long-range V2 rocket attacks started. These last, as Charles Bradley's taximan had indirectly observed, were still coming in increasing numbers. During September, only about thirty had been launched on London; in

14

November and December, the monthly figure had been about one hundred; last month, over two hundred; on present showing this February's total would be higher.

From last June a governmental order had insisted all Martha's London wards must start each night with a minimum of ten empty beds. The Senior Medical and Surgical Officers who shared overall responsibility for every admission to every bed had managed to gain exemption from this order for the six basement wards fitted into former storerooms and cavernous alcoves, but above and below ground the additional governmental order was obeyed: that, where medically possible, all air-raid casualties must be transferred out of London within twenty-four hours of admission. For over four years now, in quiet weeks, every Tuesday and Thursday morning, convoys of ambulances and ambulance coaches had made the sixty-mile southward journey to the Hut hospital on a rural hillside; in unquiet weeks, the convoys left more frequently.

Today was Tuesday, but the tidy ward bore no trace of the morning's exodus and subsequent general post to align together the remaining patients. All were bed-patients as all yesterday's 'ups' had gone in today's convoy. Their afterlunch rest-hour was over and the majority lay propped into semi-seated positions, knitting and chatting to near-neighbours, or listening to their wireless headphones. Not unusually for Alex, all nineteen women were from Martha's south-of-the-river 'zone' and had homes in tenement blocks, council flats, basement flats, two-up two-down back-to-backs, with the ubiquitous missing tiles, structural cracks, some windows boarded and those with glass, criss-crossed with dirty strips of anti-blast paper. The oldest was Miss Evers in 36, the first bed on the right from the doorway, the youngest, Noreen, in 2, the second on the left.

Miss Evers was fifty-one, and an eighth-day post-operative intestinal obstruction caused by a previously unreported and untreated primary carcinoma. The SSO [Senior Surgical Officer] had removed the growth intact in the basement theatre, Miss Evers was doing well and knitting rapidly. Noreen was sixteen, the ward pet, and was not doing – and could never do – well, being in the advanced stage of a glandular disease with no known cure. She was a slight, pale-haired, very pale girl with a pugnaciously cheerful face. She would have been transferred to the country on the day following her admission to Alex three weeks ago, had her recently war-widowed mother not refused her consent for the move. 'She's settled in nicely, Sister, and seeing Dr Roberts [the Senior Medical Officer] had to tell me there's nothing to be done but keep her happy and comfortable – he was so kind, Sister – you're all so kind and she is happy here and likes me coming in every evening and I – I like coming – and there's my job, Sister. It's so lucky that I can type and getting better at it and what I'd do without the thirty bob coming in every week, I don't know, Sister. The fifteen bob a week Army pension doesn't go far, but with two pounds five I can buy her little treats and she lives that and – and – I want her in Alex, Sister and I have to say, Sister, you're all spoiling her shocking and I'm very grateful. . . .'

Noreen lay near-flat, her eyes closed as she giggled at something on the BBC Light Programme coming over her headphones. In Bed 1, Mrs Hicks, fine-drawn, blue-veined and high propped, smiled faintly at Noreen's giggle and breathed shallowly and with the care of one that had come to terms with the fact that all human respirations have a finite number. Mrs Hicks didn't think in those words; she just knew them, instinctively.

Beyond Noreen, the medical beds stretched emptily to the terrace doors, every bed newly made-up, with its thick white cotton bedspread embossed in the centre with the Arms of St Martha, arranged with geometrical precision.

From the surgical side snatches of conversations floated to the mid-ward desk, a largish, oblong, solid mahogany table furnished with two hard chairs facing the surgicals. Snatches of exchanged family, medical and war histories; of secret recipes for reducing the tastelessness of all-vegetable Woolton Pie, and successful cake-making without butter, sugar and real eggs; of cherished knitting patterns and how to turn a pre-war summer skirt into a romper-suit for the baby. . . .

' . . . got mine rising lovely with the powdered eggs, duck, but don't never forget to use the powdered soon as it's mixed – leave the mixture sitting and turn proper nasty it can. . . .'

' . . . oh yes, Mrs Bennings, I miss my kiddies cruel same as you your twins, but like I've said all the time when they binds about being evacuees and wanting to come home – you stays safe down the country till your dad get's back – but, miss 'em? Not a day – not a night – that I don't. . . .'

' . . . no, well, dear, wouldn't expect it easy moving in with my old mum after being bombed out – never taken to my Bert, she hasn't, nor him her – but seeing he been away nigh on the five years – that's right, dear, Burma. 14th Army. Gawd Almighty's Own Division my Bert calls it in his letters always a proper card, my Bert. . . .'

'That's it, love! Five plain, one purl, first row, then three plain, three purl, second and back to five plain one purl. . . .'

Sister said quietly, 'There are occasions, Dr Brown, when I wonder if I'm running a ward or a Mothers' Union meeting.'

'I'll buy that one, Sister.' He smoothed his suede waistcoat and exchanged smiles with Mrs Bennings in 29 whose pillows were being re-arranged by Nurse Martin, the senior student nurse and Nurse Thane's great friend and setmate.

17

Mrs Bennings was a second-day post-operative appendi-cectomy whose inflamed appendix the SSO had told the theatre was the nearest near-miss to a perforation he had seen. She was a striking brunette in her mid-thirties and had been working in a munitions factory outside London since shortly after her husband joined the Army and their twins were evacuated to Devon in late 1939. Mrs Bennings had a mind of her own: having been born in Block 2, and having had her tonsils removed in Block 6, fifteen years later, she had flatly rejected the factory medical officer's advice and the arranged bed in a local cottage hospital. Instead she'd taken a train to Waterloo, stopped by at her mother's to say she was taking her belly up old Martha's, walked on and into Casualty and collapsed. In last even-ing's seven-thirty to eight, weekday visiting time, her mother said she'd done right and looked around appreciati-vely, 'Nice being back in old Alex. Not been back since Sir Joshua fetched out me gall-bladder lovely in '38 – Sir Joshua Levy's not gone, Sister? I'm ever so glad – but he'll be getting on. . . .'

Mrs Bennings, like her mother, was an old hospital-hand, so, upon accepting her returned headphones, she whispered, 'Is that doctor with the black hair your boyfriend, Nurse Martin?'

Nurse Martin, a tallish, slender, ethereal blonde, blushed in distress. 'Good gracious, no, Mrs Bennings. My fiancé's been a prisoner since Tobruk.' Then being a fourth-year and SRN [State Registered Nurse] with three-and-a-half years' wartime nursing under her white starched belt, added, 'Wasn't Sergeant Bennings at Tobruk? Didn't someone tell me he's a Gunner with the 8th?' And as she had calculated, Mrs Bennings forgot Dr Brown in her interest in her husband's war. Nurse Martin did not, which perturbed her greatly. She had loved, written regularly and been utterly faithful to the young man she had known for only a few weeks and last seen in early 1942, even though, without the tangible reminder of his photograph on her dressing-table, she sometimes had difficulty remembering what he looked like. When Sarah Thane once remarked on the photograph's slight resemblance to Dr Brown, Nurse Martin had been indignant. 'They've just both got black hair, but John's sweet and quiet and serious. Paddy Brown's only serious about medicine and if he ever stops talking it must be when he's asleep or blind drunk.' Sarah Thane, knowing Val Martin – and Paddy Brown – had dropped the subject.

'Better make tracks.' Dr Brown rose languidly. 'What's on for lunch, Sister?'

She smiled up at him, 'Pilchards without [tomato sauce], dead baby and mush [unsweetened suet pudding and unsweetened custard].'

'Mother of God.' He crossed himself and grinned. 'It's being so cheerful that keeps you going, Sister.' He drifted away, his long white coat flapping around his long, thin, narrow figure, and as always before leaving Alex stopped to exchange winks with Noreen and a few words with Mrs Hicks.

Mrs Hicks was the ward's oldest patient in time and on this occasion had been in five weeks. She was thirty-eight and for the last ten years had been in and out of Martha's medical wards with a cardiac condition consequent on untreated rheumatic fever in childhood, and as Noreen, on paper, should long have been transferred to the Hut, but had remained in Alex for roughly similar reasons. Her husband, Rifleman Hicks, had been a prisoner-of-war from the fall of Calais in 1940. Mrs Hicks still lived with her mother, aunt and grandmother in the two-up, two-down back-to-back, about one mile from the hospital, in which she had been born. She had no children and her mother and aunt visited her every weekday evening and her grandmother came every Saturday and Sunday afternoon and their visits were the high spots of her fast-shortening life.

'She knows she's on her last lap,' said Dr Roberts, the SMO, to Sister Alex and Dr Brown, the hospital's only medical registrar. 'We haven't told her, but she knows and wants to stay. If it means cooking every book to keep her, we'll cook 'em. Right, Sister? Good. Knew you'd go along.'

Downhill fast, thought Dr Brown unhappily, concealing his thoughts behind his remarkably attractive smile. He glanced covertly at the tall black oxygen cylinder in a tall black iron, low-wheeled stand on the left of her bedhead and the glass flow-meter on a high stool beside it. When in use the oxygen flowed through the humidifying meter before reaching the mask, but the long thin green rubber tubing and green rubber mask were neatly looped round the cylinder's neck. Mrs Hicks loathed wearing the mask and, as the oxygen could only ameliorate but not cure, whenever possible it was discontinued. What she needs, he thought, is a good roomy tent, but as tents roomy or otherwise for adult beds we do not have, what in hell can we do? He looked at his watch. Just about time. 'I'd best get weaving before Sister Dining-Room has me for afters. Take it easy, m'dear. Behave yourself, young Noreen.'

Noreen eased up one headphone. 'Chance'd be a fine thing, doctor!'

'Did you hear that, m'dear? What are the young coming to?' He drifted on, shaking his head and his coat flapping, through the short wide corridor known as 'the flat' that connected the ward with its main ground corridor entrance, and leaving Noreen giggling, Mrs Hicks smiling, and Nurse Martin by Bed 34 gazing fixedly, anxiously, in the opposite direction.

Mrs Bennings clasped her bandaged abdomen with both hands and, leaning towards her left neighbour, nodded towards Nurse Martin and whispered, 'Fretting for her intended, poor duck. Prisoner in Germany – can't be too healthy all the bombing day and night – not as they've not had it coming after what they give others and us – but can't be too healthy, can it?'

Nurse Thane had a vacolitre of blood under each arm and was half-way down the front stairs before she noticed the apparently bemused man leaning on a stick in the shadows of the main doors. She hurried on down and towards him. 'Lost, captain? Not to worry. Everyone gets lost here. If you want Out-patients go on to that corridor, turn left and follow the arrows. If it's the Physio Department, that's in the basement, so if you turn left or right just go down the nearest basement stairs – all off the corridor's inner wall and marked and once again, just follow the arrows and – ' she broke off abruptly not only because she had now recognised the RAMC insignia. She peered more closely up at his face. 'Excuse me, but aren't you Charles Bradley?'

He had been amused by her misconception, but that recognition surprised him too much to answer at once. She had her back to the corridor lights and in the dimness her blue-and-white striped dress looked greyish and her hair and eyes black. He recognised her fourth-year uniform and that the navy belt marked her an acting-staff nurse, but nothing else about her. 'Yes, I'm Charles Bradley.' He pulled off his beret. His short straight fair hair, cut yesterday for this morning's Board, retained most of the near-white streaks bleached by North African, Aegean and Mediterranean suns, despite nearly four months in an English hospital. 'I'm sorry nurse, but – '

'No, you don't know me, Captain Bradley.' He heard the smile in her voice and sensed rather than saw it in her eyes. 'You'd left months before my set started in September, '41. I just know you from a photo of Martha's winning the Hospitals Cup in '38 that lived on my father's study mantelpiece until he died a couple of years ago. I've got the photo somewhere in my room over the road. You were one of the backs. My brother, David Thane, was scrum-half.'

His taut face hardened and he said gently, 'I am very sorry. David was a good chap.'

'Yes. He was. Thanks.' She looked deliberately at the wooden wall. 'I remember him telling me neither of you knew who went through the window first on the night that resulted in that monstrosity. I didn't see it till '43 as from around the time they shoved it up Matron slung all first-years and second-years under 21 out of London for the duration. Been back before?'

'No,' he said. They both relaxed a little in the mutual recognition that neither would now refer again to her only and older brother killed in the desert in May, 1942. Perhaps, at some other time, they would talk of him; perhaps, never. Certainly not now in the sixth year of a war that had used up so much of their youth and amongst much else taught them the folly of looking back, or forward.

She smiled warmly. 'Welcome back to the old firm! Where'd you buy that leg?'

'Italy. D-Day dodger, that's me.'

She laughed. 'Tell that one to the Marines. Not me. Two years in wards nursing troops from Alamein, Sicily, Salerno, Anzio, Cassino — to name but a few.'

He smiled, but uncharacteristically stiffly and shyly. He was a naturally unselfconscious young man with the easy adaptability to backgrounds of those lacking the supreme egotism that is the basis of shyness. But he had altered his position to see her face more clearly and the shade of her neatly bobbed brown hair, the lines of her small uptilted face and especially her dark-lashed eyes were suddenly both strangely reminiscent of her dead brother and strangely different. And equally sudden was his disturbing sensation of being a stranger in his own hospital and to this English girl whose brother had been a great friend whom he had

22

forgotten for years and forgotten intentionally. He had been acutely saddened when he heard David Thane had been killed outright when his ambulance hit a mine outside Benghazi. But he had been as saddened too often, before and since David Thane's death; he had seen too many good chaps that had been his friends die, too many thousands of others whom he had never known, and whose mutilated bodies he had covered with the nearest blanket or piece of canvas – when there was time. Often, no time. Often, impossible to identify which limb belonged to which torso, or the torso was missing. He had had to learn to accept such things happened in war or he would crack – and there was no time for cracking in field hospitals, casualty clearing and field ambulance stations, with fellow MOs either thin on the ground or non-existent. He had long recognised that familiarity had bred not callousness but merciful amnesia, but he did not expect this girl could possibly know anything of this. It was a long time since January, 1941 and she looked so young. This must be hell for her, he thought, and determined to end it.

'Nice running into you, but I mustn't hold up that blood. Just taking a look round before a date with the Dean.'

It was not only his old friendship with her dead brother and his walking stick that made her ignore the dismissal, but both helped. They all act bloody-minded when first back after years, she thought, and at the back of her mind was grateful that the need to think objectively provided a temporary anodyne to the re-opened old wound. Even if they come straight back to UK hospitals, it makes no difference, she thought – all hospital life for patients is a kind of limbo between the old life and the new. In the old, for years overseas, they've dreamed of getting back, dating the girls they've left behind, having a pint with the chaps, walking the dog, England, Home and Beauty. . . . Then they get back and find the girlfriends have vanished into the Women's Services, Land Army, nursing, munitions, or have married other men and had the babies that are the only way out of the call-up for all women between 19 and 23 and who hadn't the heart, or guts, or both, to write them 'Dear Johns'. Nor are the chaps around for the pint; either they're away fighting, or in reserved occupations in safe areas like the wilds of Scotland or Wales, or in hospital beds, prison camps, or dead. As for the country they've come back to – it isn't the one they left behind. If they've got parents, almost invariably, they and their parents no longer speak the same language. So, in their hordes, they make for London to live it up, hit the bright spots. If they were Martha's men, they turn up here in search of old familiar faces and their lost youth and too often are disappointed on all counts and feel horribly lonely, and even worse, horribly hurt. But as they'd face a firing squad rather than admit it, they act bloody-minded. It might be different for them were this Paris, or Brussels, and still euphorically celebrating liberation. No euphoria here. Here the war's still on, uniforms are thick as dust after air-raids, and if anyone recognises their faces it's usually . . . oh, you back? Good show. Terribly sorry, must dash – see you around sometime. Cheers!

She smiled. 'No panic for this blood or I wouldn't be nattering. Just ward spares and I'm officially off. The Dean's office is still where it was in the alcove between Luke and Alex. What time's your date?'

She was so small, sweet-voiced and unaffectedly friendly that he was torn between the urge to protect her from his disturbing presence and his unexpected pleasure in her contrasting attitude to that of the former girlfriend he had rung this morning. He had not wanted to get in touch with her or any other old friends whilst in hospital, and during that period had been belatedly relieved to have no close living relatives. 'Charles who? Charles Bradley? My God, Charles – it's been years! Yes, of course, I remember you – do hold on a tick – still there? Fearfully sorry – infant shouting her head off . . . yes, naval type – married three years . . . thanks a lot! All well with you? Wizard! All the best – see you sometime . . . '

He said, 'Two-thirty. Where are you staffing?'

'Alex. Jobbing [on loan] from Cas. Where've you sprung from?'

He told her a little about his Board and the emergency military hospital near York, but nothing of his admission there last November, operations, treatment, nor of how he had been dug wounded and unconscious out of the mud as the sole survivor of a direct hit on a field ambulance station during one of the 8th Army's attacks on Highway 9 in the Po Delta last October.

She listened quietly and didn't probe for details of his wounds or war. Those two years of nursing wounded servicemen had taught her no one wanted to enlarge on either subject until he chose the moment. When it came, he talked, and the better the patient, the longer it took him to open up. And being accustomed to working in artificial and poor lighting, whilst listening, she saw plainly the clinical signs of old pain, constant nagging aches and an old, old war in the taut, strong, rather plain face that looked so immeasurably older than that of the tall, fair boy in the photograph in some drawer in her top-floor room across the road, that momentarily she marvelled at her own powers of recognition. Then she recalled how often, pre-war, her brother had pointed out to her his two especial friends in the line-up and her own, often disturbingly retentive, photographic memory. The face of David's other buddy and four more in that photograph now belonged to the dead, she reflected unhappily, and then consciously heightened her attention to Charles Bradley's face. He'd be a good patient, she noted, one of the quiet, very polite types . . . thanks, nurse, I'm okay . . . thanks, nurse, quite comfortable . . . thanks, nurse, I don't need anything (only for God's sake, nurse, get the hell out of it

25

and let me sweat it out on my own). . . .

'Have you been jobbing in Alex long?'

'Couple of weeks.' She did not explain that she had been loaned from Casualty whilst the permanent staff nurse was on unusually extended compassionate leave owing to the facts that her father had been killed by a rocket and her mother was crippled with arthritis. He'd had this war up to his back teeth, thought Sarah Thane; with luck he won't have to know about this and that; without luck, he will; but no future nor kindness in jumping the gun. 'My set were moved up here from the Hut last summer – oh, Hut make sense?' She saw it did and changed the subject. 'How much leave have you got?'

'Eight weeks.' He picked up the cue with more insight than she could appreciate. A fellow-patient in the ward he had just left had been a – to Charles – elderly Squadron Leader who had been in the Royal Flying Corps in the Great War and spent the first nine months of last year stationed near London. Early last September a flying bomb shot down by the RAF had landed on his station and put him into the hospital near York. If only 10 per cent of old Tubby's V1 horror stories were true, thought Charles, she wouldn't want to talk about this one, and yet – was it just wishful thinking or was he on the ball in sensing that right now she needed to natter – just natter pleasantly – as much as he did? If so – no, hell, how could he? She wasn't the pick-up type – so what? This wasn't a straight pick-up. She was poor old David's sister and she could always shoot him down. 'You – er – said you're off. Two-to-five?'

'Yes.' She knew what was coming, but not yet how to handle it.

'I'll probably be shot of the Dean by three and – er – if you're not booked or anything, would you care to come out and have tea somewhere?'

'Thanks, and I'm not booked, but – ' she paused to search for the right camouflage.

26

He misread her hesitation. 'Bit of a sweat having to change into civvies then back into uniform. Some other time, perhaps?'

It didn't show, but she knew she had hurt him. She wasn't having that. She said quickly, 'You've got me wrong. This isn't the frozen mitt. Just – ' She tapped her navy belt, 'wearing this it's sort of unofficial bad form to leave hospital territory for long unless on days off. We're a bit short staffed up here. But if you can make it a coffee – ' she hitched a vacolitre higher to jerk a thumb downwards 'we've that in the catacombs that you won't know about. A staff canteen, Martha's men, nurses and students, for the use of.'

He was so pleased he took it dead-pan. 'This war's gone on too long. Inter-staff fraternisation on hospital territory. Where will it all end?'

She laughed and he felt as if he had been handed a cheque for one thousand pounds. 'Don't get too lit up. Penicillin may be revolutionising surgical techniques, but inter-staff it's still the old no-touch-technique and if you were now in a white coat both our jobs would be on the line. But we are allowed to talk to each other in our canteen.'

He smiled slowly. 'Okay if I sit across the table?'

She fluttered her eyelashes. 'Come, come, captain! Table? Martha's doesn't cosset its staff with luxuries like tables, chairs, saucers, teaspoons – just as well as the joint's about four-foot square – but the coffee's not too foul, the biscuit ration comes in Tuesday mornings and this is Tuesday afternoon.'

'May I offer you a not too foul coffee and biscuits at – say – just gone three?'

'Thank you. Yes, please.'

'Great.' Suddenly, both smiled shyly. 'Whereabouts below?'

'Dead handy from the Dean's office. Just over the corridor, down the basement stairs nearest Cas.'s internal entrance, turn right and keep on till you pass the Physios. It's squeezed between their gym and Repairs and Works. And – er – in case you've forgotten, all the basement stairs are steep and slippery.'

'I won't forget, nurse. I'll take 'em slowly, nurse. Won't bust the other, nurse.'

She liked his deep quiet voice, but even more, that comeback. All good patients disliked being reminded of their physical weaknesses but accepted that sometimes this was necessary and generally did so with a smile.

'Nanny, of course, doctor, knows best. And if nanny doesn't get weaving Sister Alex'll think this blood lost for ever. Oh – my name's Sarah.'

'Charles. Thanks a lot. See you down under shortly.' He slapped on his beret and saluted. 'Cheers, Sarah.'

'Cheers, Charles,' she called over her shoulder hurrying off, turning right down the main corridor and wishing he hadn't saluted. The two young men she had loved had done so when they had said 'Cheers, Sarah,' for the last time in their lives. One of the two had been her brother, and the memories of both so disturbed her that a few seconds later she shot by the on-coming Dr Brown without noticing him or his attempts to catch her attention with a discretion necessitated by the Assistant Matron's unexpected emergence from the alcove to Matron's office several yards ahead of him.

Dr Brown cursed mentally, shrugged his hunched shoulders, dug his hands deeper into his trouser pockets, wished the Assistant Matron a civil 'Good afternoon to you, Sister,' and damned her eyes. He had always hit it off well with Sarah Thane, mainly as neither was each other's type and both knew it, and for the past two weeks he had regarded her arrival in Alex as a right turn-up for the book. She and Val Martin were such good pals that very obviously Val Martin had been bucked and not resentful to have one of her own set shoved in over her head as acting-staff nurse.

Never hurt to have a pal in the right spot, he had decided on Sarah's first day in Alex; soon as there was a breathing space, he'd take steps, but softly, softly. Little Sarah was no one's fool and that damned lovely girl Val Martin was the best damned Penelope in the business. He'd lay a year's salary that now all her exams were over she did tapestry work in the Nurses' Home over the – Mother of God! He stopped dead and flung wide his arms. 'Why's no one told me the war's over, Charlie? Will you tell me why you're not a stiff? Someone told me you'd bought it last October! To think I nearly wasted good money on another black tie!'

With a grin Charles Bradley removed the cigarette he had just lit and raised his stick in salute. On the night that he had been flattened on the flagstones of Casualty Yard, when he had eventually staggered to his feet he had promptly fallen over the prone figure of Paddy Brown, one of the final-year medical students working then as a Casualty dresser.

The two men were shaking hands when, in the doorway of the ward kitchen that lay off Alex's flat, Nurse Thane cannoned into Nurse Martin coming out with the sterile towel-covered white enamel penicillin tray that was stored in the kitchen fridge. 'Sorry, Val. My fault. Any damage?'

Val Martin carefully raised one corner of the towel. 'Flap over. Crystals, sterile water, syringes, needles, okey-dokey.' Her pretty face was masked and her trusting light blue eyes curious. 'Why are you looking all lit up?'

'Shocked at the prospect of two pints on Daisy's floor.' Daisy was Alex's wardmaid.

'She would kill you,' said Nurse Martin gently as Sister came out of the ward.

'Thank you very much, Nurse Thane. Just put them on ice and get off. Leave that tray on my desk, Nurse Martin, and get scrubbed. You'll give, I'll witness.' Sister waited and watched her patients from the ward doorway. She had already entered in the ward Penicillin Book the names of the seven patients presently on four-hourly intra-muscular injections of penicillin, collected their bedtickets (notes) from the lower footrails of their beds, and arranged them on her desk open at the prescription sheets for the simultaneous re-check by donor and witness that was made before any Martha's injection of any nature was given.

'Ah. Thanks again, Thane,' said Sister informally as they were alone. 'Sorry it took so long. Queue in the Lab?'

'No, Sister. Purely my fault as I got nattering.' Sarah hesitated and then as she liked Sister very much and knew of her constant anxiety for Major Ames and that hope was infectious, she added, 'Actually, Sister, I ran into one of my brother's old pals – same year – just out of hospital and back from slogging out four years with the 8th. I expect you may remember him. His name's – ' and there her voice was suddenly stopped by the shock of an unheralded, brilliant sheet of light that momentarily blinded her and everyone else above and below ground in the ruined hospital.

CHAPTER TWO

FAMILIARITY had bred familiarity. In the few seconds
between the speeds of light and sound, Sister reached Mrs
Hicks in 1 and Sarah Miss Evers in 36. And at one of the
mid-ward back-to-back handbasins, Nurse Martin
slammed off the elbow taps, dived wet-armed for her
nearest patient, Mrs Bennings in 29, but before she
reached the bedside the almighty roar of the newly landed
rocket's explosion swept through the hospital as if solid
stone walls and window bricks were made of thin paper.
But as, this time, the direct path of the massive blast waves
missed the standing blocks, Sister had fitted on Mrs
Hicks's oxygen mask in the further few seconds before the
second thunderous roar that was the sound of other solid
stone buildings collapsing into the huge, lethal mouth of a
new crater. When all the noise eventually faded, for a few
more seconds the only sounds in Alex were the soft hissing
of the oxygen, the gentle bubbling of the water in the flow-
meter and the sighing chorus of breath rushing back into
lungs.

Sister, with one hand on Mrs Hicks's radial pulse,
breathed deeply and smiled placidly upon her ward. 'Sorry
you've had a bit of a shock, ladies. What a good thing your
rest-hour's over. Might have woken you up.'

Noreen raised her head a few inches from her deeply
indented top pillow. 'If you ask me, Sister, gasmen be
getting ever so careless with their matches. Gasworks
blowing up all over London these days – least that's what

31

the neighbours told me before I come in here. Flying gasworks, I call the rockets.'

Her fellow students' faces were drawn with shock and fear for their families, homes, friends, neighbours and themselves, but their white lips smiled tremulously as in uniformly aged voices they agreed you couldn't be too careful with matches when you got gas, Noreen duck, and that Jerry was getting downright considerate, Sister dear.

Sarah released Miss Evers's hands and stooped to pick her knitting from the floor. Miss Evers's hands shook as she patted her short, pepper-and-salt hair before recommencing knitting very slowly. Normally her needles flashed. For the past twenty-five years Miss Evers had supported her mother and herself on her earnings as a shop assistant; she was a good worker and earned what she and her employers regarded as good money, £3 2s. 6d. per week. In her best 'little black dress', with her face powdered, she looked her age. Just then her kindly, sensible face could have belonged to a woman in her seventies.

Mrs Stamford in 35 shakily opened the powder compact she kept under her bottom pillow. She was a seventh-day post-operative strangulated abdominal hernia and currently Miss Evers's bosom friend. Mrs Stamford was 46, twice-widowed and for the last several years married to the man whose name she bore, to whom she invariably referred as 'my third' but refused to name as next-of-kin as she had not seen him for four years, didn't know where he was 'and had never what you might call taken to him.'

'Always like to check me slap after a near-miss,' she confided unsteadily to Miss Evers and Sarah. 'If I've to meet me Maker I'm meeting Him with me slap right.' She peered into the little mirror to adjust her dyed red sausage curls, ornate paste earrings and to smear on more crimson lipstick. 'Not splodged meself, have I, nurse? Look all right, do I?'

'You look wonderful, Mrs Stamford,' said Sarah truthfully, glimpsing the fear and self-control behind the beads of mascara. Sister had caught her eye. 'Be seeing you, ladies,' Sarah added and walked quietly out of the ward. In the flat she paused to put her head round the kitchen door as if suddenly recalling something she had to check in there to provide an excuse for looking back into the ward when she closed the door. She was off-duty, the patients knew it and they knew ward routine and that the sight of off-duty day staff back on-duty during their official daily three hours off was a bad sign. They know as well as we do that one's dropped in our and their backyard, she thought anxiously, watching them covertly, and as things have been dropping in the yard on and off for five years they know exactly what could have happened – and what could now be happening.

On both sides the flat was lined with doors, spare black oxygen and carbon dioxide cylinders, water and sand-filled fire buckets and stirrup pumps. The ward's only telephone was on a wall shelf just right of the open door of the dutyroom that was directly opposite the kitchen. Sarah looked at the telephone. Too soon for it to ring. After any 'major' it was usually about ten minutes before the police and ARP [Air Raid Precautions services] rang Cas. with the first warning of an inrush and then Cas. rang round the hospital. She mustn't hang about. She must get out and stay out – until she heard. But she couldn't leave them, just yet. She had only been two weeks in Alex this time but last winter for three months she had been the ward's night senior; she loved Alex and nursing the women she was watching and who had become her friends and told her of their families, anxieties, hopes and the endless corny jokes that she had laughed at as if hearing for the first time.

She heard some of them swopping them again as she watched Sister gliding placidly from bed to bed with the penicillin tray, and Val Martin looking as ever, even when

33

masked, as if she had just stepped out of a stained-glass window. No — more than ever. Beneath the thick tidy upswept roll of golden hair, Val's white forehead was strained as if her halo was too tight — a sign that Val was flapping inside. She smells a real flap, thought Sarah uneasily, and so do I. Does Sister? Who can ever tell, but she's looking my way and I must beat it. She walked slowly away from the flat and the ward half-filled with sick women telling each other you couldn't say as the view wasn't better without the houses in-between, that nearly never killed a man and that it was ever so nice to be nice and comfy in one of the ruins what Hitler knocked about a bit. She was in the ground corridor before she remembered Charles Bradley. She stopped to look both ways.

Once that corridor had run straight for half-a-mile, and connected all eight blocks and the mortuary that lay, still undamaged, at some distance beyond the rubble of Block 8. Now the corridor, reduced roughly by two-thirds, was wholly blocked by a wooden wall about twenty yards on from the wide inner entrance to Casualty that was several yards to the left across the corridor from Alex. On the far right the corridor ended some thirty yards from the outer entrance to Henry, the only usable ward in Block 5 which was on the ground floor; but at that end the wooden wall had a wide door that opened onto the temporary, unco-vered wooden ramp that ran past rubble, shells and gaps to the mortuary. The blocking wooden walls were brown and varnished; the long, stone corridor walls and ceiling were white-washed regularly, but none of the layers wholly concealed the innumerable old and new cracks especially in the riverside wall. It was lined with tall, wide, brick-blinded windows, the ubiquitous fire buckets and stirrup pumps, and doors to the terrace that were all closed and labelled in large fading scarlet: FIRE EXIT ONLY

All the corridor windows had low wide stone sills that in peacetime at this hour would have been packed with medical students gathered for the afternoon teaching rounds that had begun at two-thirty and had continued to do so down at the Hut on Mondays, Wednesdays and Fridays. On Tuesdays and Thursdays the Hut rounds began an hour earlier, as on those mornings the Professors of Medicine and Surgery, with varying numbers of honorary consultants on the Teaching Staff, went from London to the country hospital for the day. Up here, in quiet periods, the Professors, honoraries, SMO and SSO gave small teaching rounds to the ten or twelve final-year medical students spending a week in residence as medical clerks-cum-surgical dressers on a non-stop rota begun in early 1941. The students' working week started on Tuesday, as they worked predominantly as Casualty dressers and, normally, Monday was the busiest day of the Casualty week. The war had literally cut-down the hospital's bedstate, but left relatively undamaged its Casualty Department and totally unaltered the traditional habit of the Londoners in Martha's neighbourhood of regarding Casualty as their personal doctor's surgery. As the outside notices announced, the hospital was open to all patients and any requiring attention for anything from a splinter to advanced, untreated carcinoma had only to walk into Casualty Hall and say so. Being a voluntary hospital all treatment was free, and even although in peacetime it had had a private wing, since this was demolished with the rest of Block 1 by a landmine in December, 1940, Martha's had admitted no private patients. In theory, Martha's, London, remained a general hospital; in reality it was more akin to a gigantic casualty clearing station.

The only other occupants of the corridor were a short white-coated Junior Casualty Officer and two medical students in tweed jackets and brown corduroy trousers who had just emerged from the communal staff dining-room at the far end. They might know something, reflected Sarah, glancing at the alcove to the Dean's office on her immediate right. Presumably, Charles Bradley was now with the Dean and she was in an unnecessary flap. It could have landed harmlessly on an old bombsite. Some did. She waited for the trio to draw abreast. 'Any gen yet, Mr Lawson?'

Mr Lawson, one of the seven JCOs in their first six-month from qualification, blinked nervously through his moon glasses. He had not been frightened by nurses until he donned his first short white coat nine weeks ago, since when they terrified him nearly as much as the Sisters. 'Umm – er – not actually, nurse. Nothing from the cops when the SSO rang Casualty from the dining-room, but as Dacey said he didn't like the sound of the bit of hush the SSO said anyone that had finished eating should make tracks for Casualty. He'd just sat down.'

The larger, fairer student put in cheerfully, 'Hellish rowdy chap, Jerry, isn't he, nurse?'

Sarah nodded vaguely. She recognised neither student as their batch was new up last night. Being final years, they had to be at least 21, but having just heard their first rocket, they looked like excited schoolboys. She was in no mood for prep. school humour. She looked at Mr Lawson's round pink face. 'Dacey never flaps.'

'No.' Mr Lawson blinked owlishly, his nervousness forgotten. Dacey, the senior Casualty porter for the last twenty years, was the JCOs' rock and refuge.

Her mind had made itself up. 'Thanks.' She hurried on and down the nearest basement stairs.

The students turned to watch her go and wolf-whistle inaudibly. 'Who's your snappy little piece, Tom?'

Mr Lawson's mind was on Dacey. 'Thane. Jobbing in Alex from Cas. Not mine.'

'Whose?'

'Don't you chaps ever think of anything but sex?'

'What else is there to think of now the rugger season's over?'

Mr Lawson was nearly 23 and felt too old to answer. He walked on into Casualty whilst the students lingered at Alex's outer entrance to watch the distant figure of Nurse Martin pull down her mask and re-wash her hands after the final penicillin injection.

'Wow! Why do women's wards hog all the glamour, and how do we get into Alex, Dick? demanded the larger, whose name was Nigel Hastings.

Dick Dunlop, his pair – all resident students were paired – was shortish, sturdy and omniscient. 'Piece of cake. We are avid types. Soon as the old battleaxe [Sister Casualty] lets us off the chain-gang at six, we can't wait to collect case histories in Alex. The day staff are on till nine and they won't sling us out till Visitors at seven-thirty.'

'Good show.'

'Cavé. Top brass.' Dick Dunlop tipped his curly head at the little posse of white coats coming swiftly from the dining-room. 'Five bob pukka flap.'

'You're on.'

They moved on and reached Casualty only seconds ahead of the SMO, SSO, their respective and sole registrars and the Resident Anaesthetist, who wore the posse's only short white coat and was in his second sixth-month from qualification and exempt from military service as he was very short-sighted and had very flat feet.

Sarah raced down the deep, slippery stone stairs to the great, sprawling, cavernous basement that in parts dated back to the hospital's fifteenth-century foundation and had been built throughout to withstand its proximity to the Thames. Thank God for the river, she thought, from old and new habit. Only in the basement had she felt safe from the flying bombs and, whilst she realised it would provide no sanctuary from a rocket's direct hit, she shared the fairly common inter-staff conviction that it was the Thames that had so far saved the hospital from this. Current rumours insisted that the rockets were twenty times more expensive than the flying bombs and that each of the latter cost a packet and that from the way the rockets had dropped apparently indiscriminately on London, their accuracy was still unperfected and Jerry was unlikely to risk wasting all that money in the river. Please God, let this one have been wasted and me just be flapping like mad over nothing, she thought racing on.

The main basement corridor was narrow, winding, with uneven walls, ceilings and floors, lined with pipes of varying sizes and, as the main ground floor, was badly cracked. It too was regularly whitewashed and permanently lighted. But off the basement corridor were innumerable boarded-up unsafe caverns and alcoves that, being unlit and unused, cast dark shadow and chilled the atmosphere that habitually smelt of grime and must. She had long ceased to notice chill and smell, but both were new to the four medical students coming out of the staff canteen as she went in. The four stopped grumbling at the foul pong to look her over and exchange peevish shrugs. Just their luck to have to scarper when the best thing they'd seen all day showed up and they'd had the joint to themselves. But as the SSO was chucking his weight about and the chaps that moved out yesterday said he was the battleaxe's blood-brother – back to the chain-gang and odds on it was a bloody waste of good coffee.

The middle-aged canteen worker on shift alone until five o'clock paused in her mopping of spilt coffee from the small, high counter top. 'Hello, Nurse Thane! Cuppa, dear?'

'Not now, thanks, Mrs Franklin.' Sarah looked around uncertainly. Why was she so sure? And making this song and dance about letting him know? Cope with that anon. 'Can you do something for me if necessary, please?' she requested and then explained.

Mrs Franklin was delighted to have something else to

think about. That last rocket hadn't troubled her personal, seeing she'd moved in with hubby's cousins down Clapham, hubby was away at sea and both the girls safe up north in the ATS, but she'd not been able to get the old neighbours off her mind. She and hubby had been born not two good spits from the Kennington Road and had ever such a nice little council flat till it come down January of last year and she'd had to move in with the cousins. Lovely neighbours, they'd had. Didn't bear thinking now. Even down here the horrible noise rattled her ears and teeth cruel. But she liked little Nurse Thane. Been lovely to her, had Nurse Thane when that Mr Davis [the SSO] fetched out her appendix and had her in Alex last November. 'You leave it to me, nurse. If a Captain Bradley, tall, fair, with a stick comes in and you're not back I'll say he's not to wait more than the ten minutes as if you not come then it means you're ever so sorry but you've had to go back on. He'll be ever so disappointed, I'm sure.' Her pleasant, worn face clouded. 'Reckon you'll have to go back on, dear?'

'Not sure, yet.'

Mrs Franklin sighed. 'Reckon you will, nurse. I just had the SSO ringing from the dining-room. "If you got any students down there, Mrs Franklin," he says, "you tell 'em I says to get back up to Casualty stat!" ['Stat' short for the Latin 'statim'; English: at once] "What's stat?" the students say. "Well," I says, "if you young gentlemen don't know that yet you will sharpish. Say 'stat' all the time the doctors and nurses do and what it means in good English is pronto!"'

Oh God, thought Sarah. She said, 'Thanks, Mrs Franklin,' and raced off.

What was it like? What was it like to be able to make a date – to say, see you in thirty minutes – tomorrow night – next week – two weeks Sunday – and feel sure – SURE – you'd both make the date? She couldn't remember how that had felt and was still searching for the recall when her feet, apparently of their own volition, had carried her just short of the entrance to Alex and she heard its ringing telephone. She stopped as if playing grandmother's footsteps and craned for Sister's quiet voice. She heard only a few words and three seconds later was beside Sister.

Sister Alex said into the receiver, 'Thank you, Dacey. We will.' She put it down and froze Sarah's blood by turning her back to her ward. 'I'm glad you're back, Thane. You've heard.'

'Nothing specific, Sister. What did he get?'

Sister looked at her. 'The Market.'

Sarah faced the ward. She looked quickly at the floor. 'Tuesday afternoon,' she murmured without moving her stiffened lips.

'Still Market Day, sir?'

The Dean replaced the receiver of the internal telephone upon his desk and nodded briefly to Charles Bradley in the opposite chair. 'The charter King Henry VI granted the local citizens some twenty years after his granting of our hospital's charter has not yet been revoked by Parliament, Bradley, and up to this present hour their weekly street-market has been untroubled by cosmic conflagrations.'

Charles's face was expressionless and consequently harder as, without the softening play of expression, the unyielding element was very noticeable. He remembered the Market well and its traditional site in two side streets running at a right angle to each other in one of the most crowded parts of a highly populated area. 'No figure yet, sir?'

The Dean took his time. He was neat, white-haired and in his early sixties and had been too badly gassed in the Great War for further military service. He had a pedantic manner and a dry voice. 'One can expect no more than educated guesses at this early stage. Possibly between one and two hundred dead or seriously injured. Minor injured as yet unknown but no doubt will reach three figures. All the injured will, of course, have been on the periphery.'

The fair eyebrows lifted slightly. 'Of course, sir?'

'We have not, as yet, admitted one surviving casualty from a rocket's point of impact.'

'I see, sir.' He did. He pulled his folded beret from one shoulder epaulet and reached for his stick on the floor. 'I mustn't take up more of your time. Thank you for – '

'No, no, Bradley.' The Dean reached for his pipe with one thin, carbolic-soap-scented hand. 'No need to absent yourself too precipitately. Pro tem, my place is by my telephones. Very shortly those of our honoraries not today teaching in the country and upon their lawful occasions attending their patients elsewhere will be ringing to enquire if we need them here. Word travels around London with remarkable speed on these unfortunate occasions and their calls will be put through to this office. Casualty and Matron will be too occupied for such matters – so I suggest we return to our former conversation. That is – where precisely were we?'

The old boy's getting too old for this, thought Charles, lighting a cigarette, and, Christ, so am I. 'You'd just asked if my left leg would stand up to postgradding, sir. I'm sure it will; both this morning and in my final check-out yesterday I was advised to walk as much as possible.'

The Dean filled his pipe carefully. 'No more beneficial exercise, and certainly as an occasional postgraduate your pace should be leisurely. Nevertheless, though you are welcome to use as much of your leave as you see fit upon this short refresher in general medicine up here, you will be better advised to seek this in St Martha's-in-the-country. Here we are only admitting medical emergencies and with rare exceptions transferring them to the country as speedily as their conditions permit. Medical patients require quiet – and, if you will forgive an elderly physician offering you gratuitous medical advice, in my opinion a further sojourn

41

in clean, quiet, country air would benefit your general health.

'Thanks very much for the advice, sir.' Charles paused for about half a minute. He had arrived in Central Hall with an open mind on the branch of Martha's in which he would do this postgrad. if, as he anticipated, the Dean gave the necessary permission. He had then decided upon London, before Paddy Brown announced he must deal with his blood-sugar before God alone knew what was coming in, as that bastard had dropped too bloody close, and vanished to the dining-room. But Charles needed the space to recover his imagination from the Market at this moment and to slam down the mental shutters. 'May I come back to you on this, sir?'

A little of the wintery weariness at man's continuous inhumanity to man subsided from the Dean's small eyes. He approved of the man that would not be hurried and weighed every differential diagnosis before pronouncing his opinion. Spot diagnoses and swift decisions might serve well for surgeons — invaluable men, without doubt, albeit no more than skilled technicians — but the good physician took his own time. 'My dear chap, by all means. You'll always find me here and most happy to assist an old Martha's man. Not that the adjective applies in your case.'

'I'm twenty-eight, sir.'

'And no doubt regard yourself as elderly.' There was neither humour nor flattery in the dry voice. The mixture as before, reflected the Dean unemotionally. After the last war the young men came back old, and too frequently too old to learn or to appreciate their own ignorance. It was refreshing to encounter the occasional exception and could be promising — if this promise was not to be curtailed in the Far Eastern campaigns that must follow upon the ending of the war with Germany.

The ringing of his external telephone interrupted his reverie. He lowered his unlit pipe and raised the receiver.

'The Dean of – ah yes, Sir Joshua . . . yes, I fear so . . . yes, I quite agree . . . you'll inform him? Many thanks.' He rang off. 'Sir Joshua Levy ringing from Wimpole Street. Mr Masingdale has rooms below. You'll recall both – both with us, shortly. Excuse me – ' the internal telephone was ringing. 'The Dean – ah yes, Dacey?' He noted some figures on his blotter and gave Dacey the names of the incoming consultants, then put down and looked straight into Charles's steady eyes. 'First ambulances on their way. Thirty-one seriously injured and only superficially buried. Many more feared buried deeper.'

'I'll leave you to it, sir. Thank you for seeing me. I'll be in touch.'

'Good to see you back, Bradley.' The Dean came round the desk to shake hands and give Charles's left leg an openly clinical appraisal. 'Reasonably comfortable when seated?'

'Very, sir,' said Charles and they exchanged a look of total understanding that for the first time in the years of their acquaintance made Charles aware that the Dean had been an old soldier. Nothing in words; nothing on paper; nothing that had to be entered in reports. 'Thank you, sir.'

Outside the closed door a few seconds later Charles heard the muffled chimes of Big Ben striking a quarter-to-three as he stooped to slide his stick against the wall behind the nearest fire buckets. He limped on quickly to look into Casualty from its corridor entrance. From there a very broad main aisle rang straight to the main entrance from Casualty Yard that was guarded by the double rows of blast and sandbag walls that on each side jutted forward to the gap that could take three stretcher-trolleys abreast. The length of the main aisle was now lined with single files of empty stretcher-trolleys and a little group of white coats, starched uniforms and blue porters' jackets waited by the head porter's lodge that guarded the main entrance. He glanced at his watch then limped on as quickly as he could down the nearest basement stairs.

Mrs Franklin, still alone and longing and dreading to share bad news, greeted him eagerly. 'You'll be Captain Bradley, sir –' she handed on Sarah's message, then added, 'She'll not be coming down, sir. He got the Market.'

He felt himself to be absurdly pleased that Sarah Thane had forestalled the message he had intended leaving. Nice of her to want him to know she wasn't just standing him up, but she was nice – very nice. It didn't surprise him that she should have done so at a time like this, since, like Sarah, he had learnt the full value of time. Tomorrow might be another day. No one in his or her right mind would bet on it.

He said gently, 'Yes, I know. Thanks very much. If you see Nurse Thane before I do, would you thank her and say I'm sorry but had to press on.'

'Leave it to me, sir. No time for a cuppa?'

'Some other time. Someone I have to see right now.'

'Anytime Mondays to Fridays ten-to-five, sir.' Mrs Franklin looked puzzled. 'You not got a stick. Nurse said as –'

'Must've left it somewhere. Always forgetting it. Cheers for now,' he added, smiling as she looked lonely, tired and rather frightened.

'T.T.F.N., sir!' (Ta-ta For Now, a catch phrase from the wireless programme *It's That Man Again* known as ITMA.)

Lovely smile, mused Mrs Franklin, alone again and climbing back upon her high stool. On the big side for her little Nurse Thane with the eyes, but a nice proper young gentleman. He'd do. She looked at her knitting in a string-bag on an under-counter shelf. Hadn't had the heart to touch it after Mr Black from Repairs and Works put his head in to say the Market had it. Tuesday and all – didn't bear thinking. She looked at the gently simmering urns, the rows of clean mugs, today's new biscuits bag, the solitary teaspoon on a long narrow chain bolted to the counter, and then up at the lowish, steamy, whitewashed

44

uneven ceiling. Right under Cas. Hall, she was, but deep, too deep to hear what was going on up there and, till the next come in, nothing to do but think. When there was nothing more you could do, keeping the hands busy helped a mite.

She took out the sweater she was knitting in oiled-wool for her merchant seaman husband. She was still sitting knitting upon her high stool and waiting for her next customer when her shift ended and she closed the canteen at five o'clock.

CHAPTER THREE

'WHERE do you want her, Sister?' Nigel Hastings's query had become mechanical and his voice a little breathless. He hoped to God Sister Alex would get a move on as this poor old biddy weighed a ton. He held the head poles and Dick Dunlop the foot of the laden stretcher in the ward doorway. It was the eighteenth to come into Alex in the last two hours and the ninth that had had to be carried after the use of stretcher-trolleys to ground-floor wards had had to be withdrawn.

Sister Alex, masked and with her sleeves rolled above her elbows, bent over the comatosed woman under the thick, grey, Casualty blankets. The woman was still in her own torn clothes that were coated with thick grey dust as were her hair, face and whole body. The one shoe she had worn on admission to Casualty lay on the top of the blankets at one side of her feet; safety-pinned to the top blanket above her chest was a large white cardboard War Emergency Admission's label. It had been filled-in and signed by the SMO and beneath the date, time of Casualty admission, and listed drugs there given and in hand for ward use, read: V2 cas. [casualty]. UNKNOWN FEMALE. Age approx 40. NO hge/int. inj./fracts. [haemorrhage/internal injuries/fractures]. SHOCK plus Mult. lacs. [Multiple lacerations]. Admit ALEXANDRA.

Nurse Martin swiftly removed the shoe and momentarily disappeared to label and deposit it in the single bathroom that was next to the dutyroom, whilst Sister checked the woman's pulse, skin temperature and general condition. The filthy dust clung to Sister's fingers and was smeared on the damp shirts and glistening faces of the two students. All the stretcher-bearers were now medical students as the experienced porters, all too old, young, or physically unfit for military service, were too valuable to be spared from Casualty and the theatre. And all Alex's admissions this afternoon so far had arrived without notice, as none were on the Dangerously Ill List. On these occasions Casualty only forewarned the wards of in-coming DILs.

Nigel Hastings tightened his grip on the poles, glanced over one shoulder to watch Sister gently raising in turn the closed eyelids, felt the sweat trickling down his nose and thought, old Dacey wasn't kidding.

Dacey briefed the students when the trolleys ran out. 'Each'll be heavier than the last and head's the heaviest, so that end's for the strongest. Take 'em slow and steady. Watch there's no tipping round corners and don't forget head first for all but stiffs. When you get to the ward stop, same as with the trolleys, to ask the Sister which bed. When you get to the bed, set 'em down careful. Had enough shock for the one day they have. Once down, nip out the poles careful then step aside for the nurses to get the canvas out from under, then nip canvas, poles and yourselves back here, pronto! Coming in faster now the cops've closed our road to all but trams, official traffic and walking-injured or searchers. Sooner those that can get to beds get there, best for all.' He glanced around the great oblong hall off which lay a rabbit-warren of small, open-doored clinical and surgical dressing-rooms and that had, on either side of the main aisle, rows of long, pew-like mahogany benches. In the little rooms, and against the hall walls on all sides, were grouped pairs of stretcher-trolleys filled with grey-faced figures huddled under grey blankets and each with either one arm or leg outstretched in a plaster-of-paris back

47

splint. Every pair shared a white metal, portable transfusion-cum-drip infusion stand, whose tall, slender white pole bore the crimson and white oblong glass bottles that sprouted long thin red rubber tubes to which were attached the wide-bore needles or glass canulae strapped into veins in the outstretched limbs. The benches were already crowded with slumped, seated, dusty, shocked figures that were the minor injured that had managed to stagger in for help unaided and would be numbered only by Casualty. Throughout this war, after civilian air attacks the official governmental figures only gave the numbers of the seriously injured and known, but not always identified, dead. 'War's good as over, some says,' Dacey observed laconically. 'Seems Jerry's not heard. And here we go again – ' he dismissed the students with a thumb jerk to attend a trio of distraught, searching relatives suddenly hovering by the lodge. 'You'll be wanting Sister Casualty,' he told them kindly. 'Sister'll know best where to look – step this way please.'

It was just under three hours since Sarah's return to Alex had been followed within minutes by that of Nurse Yates, a third-year, Daisy the wardmaid, and Nurse Burton, the second-year and ward junior, from her prematurely ended lecture. Nurse Burton had been off from ten-to-one this morning, but Nurse Yates, as Sarah, had a two-to-five and Daisy a one-thirty-to-four-thirty. Authority had never requested the immediate return to duty of all off-duty day staff for major emergencies; the automatic and total voluntary response was uniformly accepted as part of the natural order of wartime life. When possible, the lost off-duty was later made up; when not, it was forgotten. The only presently absent member of Alex's staff was Nurse Grey, the more senior third-year, whose weekly day off was Tuesday and who had last evening gone home to Guildford.

The completed staff gathered around Sister at the desk,

the nurses standing in order of seniority with their hands correctly held behind their backs. Daisy stood by Nurse Burton. Daisy's pink-cotton-sleeved arms were folded over her ample breast to mark her independence and long service.

Sister said placidly, 'Thank you all for coming back. Nurses Thane and Martin, emergency routine, please. Just get up five emergency beds from the terrace end for the present. Thank you, nurses.' She turned to Nurse Yates as the two seniors vanished. 'Normal routine for you and Nurse Burton, please. I've made your lists of washings, dressings and beds that, of course, you'll do together. Nurse Burton, you must help Nurse Yates with the lifting, and as usual, Daisy, with teas and suppers. If either of you are needed with the emergency routine, either I, or Nurse Thane, will tell you. Thank you, nurses.' She smiled at Daisy. 'Thank you again for coming back. Teas round at the usual three-thirty for all on today's lunch list only, please.'

'I'll have 'em out on time, Sister. Knew you'd need a hand,' allowed Daisy. She was youngish and comely and wore her starched white mob-cap precariously skewered on tight rows of peroxide blonde curls and a belligerent expression. She had been Alex's wardmaid since 1935 and firmly refused an offered transfer to the Hut on the grounds that she liked a bit of life and couldn't be doing with all that quiet down the country. She particularly liked spending a couple of hours in the Market on Tuesday afternoons with her friend Mavis, the Rachel Ward ward-maid, with whom she shared a ground-floor room in the Nurses' Home. Been along there this afternoon, brooded Daisy, if Mavis's corns had not been playing up. Given them a proper turn when they heard. Mavis said it hadn't been Meant. Daisy didn't know about that, but she knew what this meant to her Alex and it wasn't right. 'Large pot'll be brewing when wanted, Sister,' she added shortly.

She bustled off to what she – and all Alex – regarded as her kitchen and, having closed the door, she began filling the hot water urn and softly singing 'You Are My Sunshine.'

When that eighteenth stretcher paused in the doorway, the ward's largest brown metal teapot brewing on an asbestos mat over a low ring on the gas cooker had twice been refilled. The tea had been drunk by some of the searching relatives in the bathroom across the flat that was temporarily converted into a relatives' rest-cum-identification room by Sarah and Val Martin after they had put up the emergency beds. That bathroom had initially been installed for the ward sister's private use in the era when she had lived in her ward and the dutyroom had been her bedroom. The last had been properly converted when that era ended, in Martha's, shortly after the Great War; the bathroom was left unaltered. For its conversion under emergency routine, fracture boards were laid across the end half of the old-fashioned, high, claw-footed bath, two hard chairs and a small table were brought in from the dutyroom, and left on the table was a tray set with six clean medicine glasses, a covered jug of drinking water, the large stock bottle of sal volatile, small stock bottle of brandy, and a clean tea-towel. By the time Nurse Martin deposited the eighteenth admission's single shoe labelled E.B. (Emergency Bed) 37 on the fracture boards, they held a small stack of shoes, some single, some paired, and all too dust-engrimed to expose their real colours. And in the bath were a smaller number of equally dusty but also blood-matted outdoor coats and jackets that had had to be cut off in Casualty to expose what lay beneath; as the shoes, the garments were only labelled with bed numbers and could prove useful guides to the identification of their owners. All British civilians had National Identity cards, but women generally carried these in their handbags and not pockets. No handbags had yet come in, nor were expected to do so before, at the earliest, tomorrow morning. The

50

rescue squads digging against the clock had no time for salvaging personal possessions; when found, these were flung aside in heaps to be removed and sorted later; later still they would be delivered to the hospitals where it was known, or suspected, the owners had been warded. Sometimes it was two or three days before the handbags reached the wards, but invariably, unless emptied by the explosions, their contents were as intact as when the bags had been blown or dropped from their owners' hands.

No sal volatile or brandy had yet been needed, partially as the emergency was comparatively young and partially as none of Alex's presently admitted casualties was grossly injured. Those in this category had gone either to Rachel or Mark, the acute female and male surgical wards in the basement and nearest the theatre, or were still on stretcher-trolleys in Casualty being transfused, or in the theatre-queue in the anaesthetic room, or upon operating tables, or had died in Casualty and their bodies were in refrigerators in the mortuary.

The theatre, opened in the basement from late 1940, had five tables, a long dark green linen curtain for an outer wall and a wholly curtained area roughly ten-foot square for an anaesthetic room. The surgeons' and theatre nurses' changing-rooms were in curtained-off former storerooms fitted with handbasins, rows of pegs, a few open deal lockers, fewer hard chairs and little else. Now, in the theatre proper, all five tables were in action; every operating team worked within touching distance of the next table, but the crowding was less acute than it might have been owing to the reduction of the teams. Each had one leading surgeon, one surgical assistant, one instrument nurse, one anaesthetist and, with one exception, a half-share in one 'dirty' nurse. The bare-handed 'dirty' was the liaison between the sterile gowned and rubber-gloved team and such items as steriliser lids, saline cauldron taps, mechanical sucker and X-ray screen switches, amongst countless others. The exceptional table was Sir Joshua Levy's that had Sister Theatre combining 'dirtying' with supervising her entire theatre and the four casualties waiting on stretcher-trolleys in the anaesthetic room. Three other leading surgeons, and four anaesthetists were elderly honorary consultants who had rushed back to offer their help very shortly after Sir Joshua and Mr Masingdale. The last, with the SSO and the Resident Anaesthetist, were still working in Casualty. The Surgical Registrar led at the fifth table and his anaesthetist was Charles Bradley, whom the steam from the bubbling sterilisers and heat from the powerful overhead table lamps were constantly reminding of Sicily in the summer of 1943. Even the same mingled smell of ether, anaesthetics, fresh-spilled blood and dust. But one big difference. The patients. Not one young or youngish soldier. All civvies, and mostly women. He turned his dark green linen-capped and masked head for another of his repeated checks on the gauges and taps of his anaesthetic machine and glanced briefly at the other tables. As he turned back to the face of the woman under the anaesthetic mask his left hand held in place, with his third finger permanently on one of her temporal pulses, his own face beneath the damp green linen mask wore a grimness it had often worn in battle areas, but never before in his own country.

The eighteenth stretcher, escorted by Val Martin, moved slowly up the ward to Sarah waiting by E.B. 37, the nearest to the terrace end of the five beds in single file down the middle of the ward. Sister stayed in the doorway, watching her ward, waiting for the next unannounced stretcher, telephone call, and 'Looking for my mum – my aunty – my sister, Sister, and that big Sister down Casualty said to try Alexandra first – have you got her, Sister? Oh – oh, yes, you'll need to know – Mrs Joan Mary Thomas, Sister – age – oh – fifty-odd – stoutish – black hair going grey like — have you got her, Sister? HAVE YOU GOT HER?'

Sometimes, 'Oh, thank Gawd, Sister — yes — that's mum's old coat — you got her! Oh, thank Gawd —' then, a little later, 'Ta, Sister, ta — needed that cuppa — oh thank Gawd —' and then, always, 'Sister, she — she is going to be all right?'

As often, 'No, Sister, no — swear blind none of them's hers — yes, ta — just take a look —' and then, 'No, Sister, no — she's not one of them — no, ta ever so — won't stop for the cuppa — try Luke next down the corridor? Yes — do that — ta, Sister — sorry to have troubled you. . . . '

Whilst waiting for Sister's 'E.B. 37 please, gentlemen,' Nigel Hastings had winked at Noreen. Mrs Hicks, off oxygen, waited for the stretcher to go by before whispering, 'I see him giving you the glad eye, duck! You best watch yourself —' she had to stop for breath 'Noreen — always getting glad eyes from the students' another pause 'and what your mum'd say I'd not like to think!' She made Noreen giggle and was glad. Not nice seeing all this at her age — got to keep her chin up. Mrs Hicks smiled conspiratorially across at Miss Evers. Miss Evers smiled back, determinedly brightly. Like most of her follow 'olds' up the surgical side, she knitted as if her life depended upon her finishing her row and kept a covert watch on the doorway for the next stretcher, next appearance of those searching singly or in pairs from ARP Wardens' Posts to hospital, and often hospital after hospital and ward after ward for those they loved, or just liked, or had tolerated, accepted as neighbours that kept themselves to themselves and who they knew had gone along to the Market this afternoon and not returned home.

No one knitted in the medical side or the four beds backed against the terrace wall. Mrs Hicks and Noreen were too ill for the exercise and all the rocket's victims were still in semi-shocked, semi-medicated comas, with the feet of their beds uniformly uptilted and foot castors locked into high wooden bedblocks. They lay very still, and the greyness of their untidy hair and closed, sunken, ageless faces was accentuated by the whiteness of their single soft pillows and top bedclothes laid over iron bedcradles to keep the weight off the bruised, lacerated bodies still in day clothes under loosely arranged grey blankets. The immediate ward treatment of air raid casualties had long been radically altered from that in the early years of the war; it had been proven that the less casualties were touched whilst still under the shock, the swifter was eventual recovery. So where individual injuries permitted, they were touched as little as possible and only very gently until they surfaced of their own accord which could take from under one to many hours. It was only then that they were blanket-bathed, their hair washed, superficial wounds dressed and bodies reclothed in clean, split-back nightgowns. Throughout the comatosed period, the less seriously injured were on fifteen-minute pulse checks and the more seriously on ten-minutes. The special pulse charts hung immediately beneath the white cardboard labels topping the clean, blank bedtickets hanging from the lower front footrails of their uptilted beds; above these beds hovered filmy grey clouds that darkened the white china shades of the lights hanging from the high ceiling, turned orange the glowing bulbs. Neither the size of the huge ward nor the wartime installed ventilation system could properly disperse the dust.

Nurse Yates lifted from a stack two wooden-framed, red cotton-sided, fixed-footed screens, supported them in the approved position under her right arm and upon her right hip, and glanced indignantly at the moving stretcher. Nurse Yates was 22, slim, sharply pretty and given to taking umbrage. She had taken it with Jerry for disrupting her afternoon plans to wash her auburn hair, with Sister for putting her on normal and not emergency routine, with

Nurse Thane for swanning round in a staff nurse's belt though only half-way through her fourth year, with Nurse Martin for not being browned off because one of her set had ben hoicked from Cas. over her head and, above all, for being prettier than herself, and with Nurse Burton for being such a cocky know-all and never remembering she, Nurse Yates, was eight months senior and that she, Edwina Burton, was no longer head girl of Rolvenden and was instead that lowest form of hospital life, the ward junior. Just her luck, fumed Nurse Yates, to be landed with washings, dressings, beds, TPRs (temperature, pulse, respirations) and medicines for the 'olds' whilst Thane and Martin were having all the fun doing all the really interesting nursing.

'Sorry to break up the knitting, Miss Evers. Washing time.'

'Just ready for a nice wash, Nurse Yates. Feel a bit messy. You know how it is.'

Nurse Yates didn't. She had never been a hospital patient and had little imagination. But as she was exceptionally efficient and was being well trained, she knew what to say. 'Oh yes.' She opened the screens round Miss Evers's bed. 'Getting rather hot in here.'

'No wonder, all the coming and going, nurse.' Miss Evers's voice was hushed as if in church and the lines of her kindly, sensible face were deepened by her anxiety for her mother. Mrs Evers hadn't been along to the Market for years, but as Miss Evers had earlier confided to Mrs Stamford, there was no telling what elderly folk would take a notion to doing and there wouldn't be anyone to step down to the box on the corner and give her a tinkle till Mr Hall from next door got home from work and stepped in with the evening paper. Mrs Hall couldn't be a better neighbour, but she didn't like telephones. Bothered her, Mrs Hall said. Mrs Stamford had said it took all sorts and like they said, no news was good news. Miss Evers hadn't liked to mention times it was and times it wasn't, seeing

55

then Mrs Stamford hadn't had the tinkle from her neighbour saying their building got no worse than a good shake-up. Miss Evers now reminded herself that Mr Hall would soon be home from work and it wasn't right just to fret for her own with all those poor souls lying on their heads opposite and more to come she'd be bound. But not trusting her voice to talk of the casualties yet, she substituted, 'The poor young students, getting ever so tired, nurse. Only got to look.'

Nurse Yates smiled perfunctorily and neatly folded and hung Miss Evers's quilt on her top footrail. Nurse Yates had neither interest nor sympathy for any man in London. ('Any man' to Nurse Yates was Martha's man.) This last January she had taken great umbrage with Matron for moving her set up from the Hut a couple of days after her first date with the junior gynae houseman that had resulted in their playing footy in the flicks. The air in that cinema had been as stuffy as Alex now, she recalled, streaking for the sluice that lay off the corridor running from the ward's left far end, for washing bowl, rubber mat, mouthwash mug and bowl. Flipping typical of Jerry! First he blew out all the windows so they had to be bricked-in, then he filled the ward with foul dust that made her eyes smart and would force her to wash her hair tonight when everyone else would be washing theirs and the water in the Home would be cold as flipping charity.

Sister stopped the departing students in the doorway. 'Any idea how many waiting to come to us?'

'Sorry, Sister, no.' Dick Dunlop propped a heavy pole on one aching shoulder. 'Cas. was still bursting at the seams when we left, but old Dacey said there could be a bit of a holdup for the ground floor wards whilst the chaps are digging deeper.' His dust-reddened eyes blinked at the medical side. 'Feet up to boost blood-pressure, blood to the brain and so on?'

'Yes, Mr — ?'

'Dunlop, Sister.' He jerked a thumb. 'Hastings.'

Nigel Hastings, a pole on one shoulder, canvas on the other, mopped his face with a greyed handkerchief. 'Always out cold, Sister?'

'Being buried alive whether injured or not, is a very clinically shocking experience, Mr Hastings.'

'Must be. Er – how long'll they keep coming, Sister?'

'On past showing, into tomorrow morning. The squads will go on digging much longer. They'll keep on until convinced no one's left alive, but inevitably, the longer it takes to find them the greater the chances that some alive at this moment will have died of shock, haemorrhage, asphyxiation or just plain terror before they're reached.' The students stared at her. 'Thank you, gentlemen,' she prompted and, as they walked off toting the poles like fishing rods, she caught Sarah's eye.

Sarah gently removed her fingers from the newcomer's limp, clammy wrist. 'Sister wants me. Take over pulses, Val.' And seeing the sudden widening of Val's eyes, murmured quickly, 'All beginning to pick up.'

Val Martin nodded apprehensively. She was a very conscientious, and kind, nurse, but responsibility secretly terrified her – as she and her set knew and her nursing authorities suspected. When so terrified, she lost her professional nerve and, whilst she could still be relied upon to do exactly as told, became incapable of telling others what to do. She knew this flap was making her panic madly inside and she glanced with an uncharacteristic touch of envy at her friend's swiftly retreating back. Why couldn't she be like Sarah and sure of herself and not sick with fear that she would mis-count a pulse, miss a sudden variation in volume or rhythm, or the first signs and symptoms of a sudden deterioration in an unconscious face? She shouldn't miss anything. She knew exactly what to watch for. When there was no flap on having spent years taking pulses, she could time any to within two seconds' accuracy without a

57

watch like all her set. The others didn't fall apart inside. Why did she? She wasn't nearly as frightened of the rockets as she had been of the doodlebugs and she wasn't frightened of Sister Alex. She didn't know the answers. She had forgotten her remarkably sheltered upbringing as the only, beloved child of fairly wealthy, relatively elderly and over-protective parents and that her decision, at nineteen, to start training in Martha's had been the first she had ever made for herself.

'Yes, Sister?'

'If those boys are right, temporary lull, Thane.' Sister pulled down her mask and looked at the last four empty beds. 'Won't last. Take over here. I must go all round then we'll put up our last five emergency beds. Tell Burton to get ready the clean linen now to save time. She's in the kitchen.'

Sarah put her head round the kitchen door. Daisy, still softly singing 'You Are My Sunshine', was transferring to the pre-warmed oven a large dish of shepherd's pie from the unplugged electric food trolley she had just collected from the main kitchen, and broke off to snap, 'Supper's not due in till six and only just gone quarter-to, Nurse Thane.'

'No panic, Daisy. Just scrounging Nurse Burton for a couple of minutes,' Sarah said, and then quickly explained why to the tall, striking brunette laying out cutlery on the top shelf of the large wooden tea-cum-drinks trolley with the assurance of a dowager duchess. Nurse Burton was twenty-one and, in her own opinion, a born Matron of Martha's.

'Right, nurse!' Nurse Burton smartly removed herself to the linen room across the flat.

'Hold it a tick, Nurse Thane. How they doing?'

'Picking up slowly, Daisy.'

Daisy nodded belligerently and recommenced her song. Sarah glanced at her in silence and then closed the door. She couldn't hear Daisy's voice from the flat, but the unheard song darkened her eyes to deep violet. Daisy always sang in

58

her kitchen and her choice of song was good as a ther-mometer. When she's happy, thought Sarah, it's 'I Don't Want To Set The World On Fire'; when browned-off, 'Don't Fence Me In'; and when she wants to weep, 'You Are My Sunshine'. Daisy and me, she thought watching the ward, Daisy and me. But the telephone was ringing.

'Alexandra Ward. Staff nurse speaking.'

'Outside call for you, nurse. Through to the ward now, caller − staff nurse on the line.'

'Mr Hall, Miss Evers's neighbour here, Staff − just to let Miss Evers know as the old lady's nicely and Mrs Hall's been with her since he dropped it. No damage down our street but got hisself a proper bullseye this time, I can tell you, Staff − can't see for smoke and dust and hundreds gone, they say. You'll be busy, eh?'

'Quite busy, Mr Hall. Thank you so much for ringing. Miss Evers'll be most grateful. I'll tell her now and I'm so glad all's well down the street.'

'Weight off my mind when I got back from work I don't mind saying, Staff. Well, I mean, never know what you'll find when you get back, do you? Much obliged.'

'Thank you, again, Mr Hall.' She rang off, hurried in with the good news, and had just returned to the doorway when a man in soot, dust and water-drenched fireman's uniform charged into the flat tugging off his helmet. His face was so streaked with black that the mopped white patches round his blood-shot eyes made him look like a badly made-up clown. 'Who are you looking for, Fireman?'

'It's the wife, nurse − I didn't know she'd gone along the Market till one of my mates said he saw 'em lifting her out and reckoned she come up Martha's and that big Sister along Casualty said try Alexandra −' the words rushed out and he grabbed and shook her arm. 'Have you got the wife, nurse? HAVE YOU GOT HER?'

She patted his filthy clutching hand and said gently, 'Tell me what your wife looks like and her age, Mr −'

'Foster, nurse. She's Dora – oh – I'm ever so sorry –' He let go and nodded unhappily at the black smears on her arm.

'Couldn't matter less, Mr Foster. Now, Mrs Dora Foster. Age?'

'Oh, I dunno – yes – yes – thirty and – and small like same as you and – yes – your sort of hair and little face – have you got her, nurse?'

Sarah's mind gave an almost audible click, but she had to be careful. Nothing at these moments was more cruel then the raising of a false hope. 'Just come into this bathroom one moment, Mr Foster.' She half-ushered, half-pushed him in and onto a hard chair. 'We have admitted a small lady who could be your wife's age and was wearing this outdoor coat. Is it Mrs Foster's?'

He sat on the edge of the chair, his helmet on the floor, his reddened eyes glazing with urgency. 'She's just got the blue tweed, nurse – just the one – that's not blue –'

'I'm not so sure. Wait.' She swung the bath's remaining contents onto the fracture board and held the end of one torn sleeve under the running cold tap. 'This is tweed and I think – yes, blue – look! And how about these coat buttons – little anchors on them – recognise them?' She saw the hope flare in the agonised face. 'Mrs Foster's?' He could only nod. Thank God, she thought, thank God I can be honest. 'Yes. She's in Bed 11 and though very shocked not too hurt. I'll take you to her in one moment.' She quickly poured a dose of sal volatile and diluted it with water and put the medicine glass in his hand. 'Sip that, Mr Foster. Don't gulp or it'll choke you. That's it. Good.' She helped him up and, holding his arm, led him up the ward and then had to leave him with Val Martin as the telephone was ringing. She watched him whilst raising the receiver. Val had seated him on his unconscious wife's bedside locker and the tears pouring down his face were making white streaks.

'Alexandra Ward. Staff Nurse speaking.'

'This is Sister Casualty, Nurse Thane. . . . '

Sarah stiffened, and as she listened her face was averted from the ward and suddenly as white as the mask limp round her throat. She put the phone down as Nurse Burton pushed a neatly loaded linen-trolley from the linen room that was next door down from the bathroom.

'I say – that is, excuse me, Nurse Thane, but are you all right?'

'Yes, thanks, Burton,' lied Sarah. 'Wait.' She caught Sister's eye then turned back to the tall junior. 'This gen is staff only. If patients ask, act dumb. Cas. are sending us a DIL child soon as they've got the blood running in. All veins collapsed. SSO's now doing a cut-down. UNKNOWN. Age approx. twelve.'

Nurse Burton had paled. She had three younger sisters. 'Why was she here and not evacuated?'

'No one knows.' Sarah heaved from the wall one of the spare oxygen cylinders already locked into a wheeled stand as she spoke. 'Ask Daisy from me to start suppers early. Distract attention.' Sister had arrived. 'DIL, Sister. Little girl. . . . '

Nurse Burton returned her trolley to the linen room, shot over to the kitchen and closing the door, momentarily leant against it. 'Flap on, Daisy –'

'You're telling me, nurse!'

'No, I mean, new flap,' said Nurse Burton unsteadily. The news and the sight of the acting-staff nurse she had previously mentally categorised as the right type looking about to pass out, had stripped off the self-assurance she had had to keep mentally boosting all afternoon. It was only two weeks since, with the seven oldest members of her second-year set, she had been transferred to London from one of the Emergency Medical Service hospitals in rural southern England that had a nursing unit from Martha's. There she had nursed wounded servicemen and flying bomb and rocket casualties from London, but none had come in newly injured in their own torn, dusty, blood-stained clothes. Unlike Nurse Yates, Nurse Burton had been thankful to be on normal routine, and whenever she was in the ward she had felt guilty about the way she had avoided looking at the admissions that to her looked neither like patients nor women. Just lying there like logs covered in muck, she had thought guiltily, then she told herself that if she didn't press on regardless she would never get her routine finished on time and how Sister Preliminary Training School always said that routine was the structure that upheld the ward and in all circumstances must be done properly and upon time. . . . Any nurse can rise to an exceptional occasion, nurses. The good nurse rises to all occasions and never lowers her standards.

Normally Nurse Burton enjoyed rising to occasions, just as she had enjoyed her training – so like school – until this afternoon. Alex had turned into a place that was nothing like school and had a horrid sort of smell she had never smelt before and that wasn't just the dust, though that was bad enough. But she couldn't identify what 'it' was, as this was her first encounter with the ugly scent of human fear now beginning to emanate from the subconscious and few semi-conscious minds of the patients that had been buried alive and whose faces would soon seem beaded with black oil as the sweating that accompanied the return of memory forced the grime from their facial pores.

Five minutes later the long flex of the electric food trolley was plugged in between 29 and 28 and the wooden trolley parked just beyond. Daisy, with sleeves buttoned to the wrist, dished up, whilst Nurse Burton, her mask in her dress pocket, went from bed to bed with the serving tray. Emergency Bed 40, the nearest to the desk, waited empty behind red screens, stripped to its hot water bottle heated bottom sheet to receive a stretcher, the top bedclothes in a neat, quickly unfolded pack on the seat of the hard chair serving as bedside locker. Over the back of the chair, an iron bedcradle; under the bed, pairs of bedblocks in rising heights; and in their appointed places around the bed, oxygen and carbon dioxide apparatus, portable transfusion stand, and the double-glass-shelved emergency sterile dressings, transfusion and hypodermic trolley, that all the 'olds' but Miss Evers had in silence watched being wheeled into the screened area, and then in silence exchanged glances.

Big Ben had just struck six when they watched Nurse Thane emerge from those screens to join Sister in the doorway, disappear with her into the flat and then in seconds re-appear on either side of the stretcher-trolley moving without pause to the screened bed, Miss Evers's 'washing' screens hid the little procession from her; the positioning of Sister and Sarah hid from all the watchers the size of the figure under the grey blankets and temporarily covered outstretched left arm. Dr Brown, masked and in rolled-up shirt sleeves, walked with one hand under the covers over the arm, and his other held above his head the connected vacolitre of whole blood.

Mrs Stamford watched until the screens were closed swiftly round E.B.40, then she shook her red head at her thoughts and lowered untasted the shepherd's pie on her fork. Quite nice, this evening, got a real taste of mince, but just couldn't stomach it, she decided, until she saw Noreen's raised head and frightened eyes. She smiled brightly at Noreen and forced the unwanted forkful into her crimson-smeared mouth. she swallowed and stage-whispered, 'Good pie this, duck. You'll like it.'

The soft rumble of the stretcher-trolley's rubber wheels alerted Nurse Yates and heightened her indignation over not having been warned suppers were starting early. Flipping typical! Just like Thane to be too snooty to tip her off a DIL was coming in. She peered over Miss Evers's screens, glimpsed the unconscious childish face that had been sponged clean in Casualty and bit her lower lip. Was the mother clean round the bend? Didn't she realise kids must stay out of London until all the launching-pads had been mopped up? Hadn't she eyes — ears — and where was she? Where was someone? A kid that age couldn't have been on her own — but — yes — of course — oh, how flipping awful! Still, stupid to get all worked-up — only somehow — you just couldn't not get all worked-up when they turned out to be kids.

She turned back to Miss Evers and lied efficiently, 'Flap's slackening. Using stretcher-trolleys again. Comfortable? Good-oh. Let's get you cleared away for your nice supper.'

In the silence behind the screened E.B.40, the stretcher was laid upon the bed as if made of eggshells. The trolley porters, again Nigel Hastings and Dick Dunlop, stood back whilst Sister and Sarah, working from either side of the bed, carefully eased under their hands to raise the child the couple of inches necessary for Val Martin to slide out the canvas and Dr Brown hung the blood on the hook of the waiting pole. The little girl was sturdy, well-grown, well-clothed and her wrists and small cold hands were healthily chubby. She had short straight hair that was probably light brown, but the few strands lying across all that was visible of her bloodless forehead were dark grey. All that was visible, because the green rubber oxygen mask hid so much of her small face and looked an obscenity to all round her bed. And the fluttering little green rubber bag attached to the base of the mask looked as if it had entrapped a dying butterfly.

Dr Brown, hitching on his stethoscope, jerked his grey-black head at the students. They dragged their mesmerised gazes from the fluttering bag to disappear with their trolley, avoiding the patients' and each other's eyes, and trying to avoid their own thoughts and immediate reaction upon discovering. Damned lucky to be in on one before the show was over, they'd agreed, and privately the prospect had eased a little of their old, never mentioned, war-long guilt. Their entire war to date had been spent at school, university and Medical School in areas beyond the range or interest of enemy bombing planes and machines. For years their lack of uniforms had secretly bothered them, especially when travelling around a country in which all their contemporaries of both sexes seemed to be in uniform. They had continuously consoled themselves with the reflections that if any chaps were essential to the war it was the chaps that knew how to stick the pieces together again and had said chaps couldn't qualify overnight. Once qualified, they'd do their stuff – know all the answers.

All? After old Josh Levy in Cas. just now. Old Josh, the finest surgeon in Martha's and many said all England, whom the SSO had hoicked up from the theatre. 'I'm sorry, Mr Davis – very sorry – nothing I can do for this poor little lass. Nothing any surgeon on God's earth can do for her now. If I dared touch her – and I dare not – the shock and also the anaesthetic would kill her in minutes. Where are you sending her? Yes, Alex is the nearest for her family if – dear, dear, dear – anyone else you'd like me to see whilst I'm above ground? Woman in Room 10? Right. . . . '

'Doorway, pro tem. please, Nurse Martin.'

'Yes, Sister.' Val Martin backed away quietly, torn between distress and gratitude that the nursing of the illest patient was the traditional responsibility of the most senior ward nurse. As she backed, for a fraction of a moment her distressed eyes met those of Dr Brown and, for that fraction of a moment, both felt comforted.

Sister was still at the child's bedside when Nurse Burton, hurrying from the kitchen as the telephone started ringing, saw Nurse Martin standing in the bathroom comforting in her arms a weeping woman. Nurse Burton said softly, 'I'll cope, nurse,' and did. A few seconds later

65

she slid between the red screens. 'Please Sister, Matron would like to speak to you on the telephone.'

'Thank you, nurse.' Sister shot Sarah a look that said, 'We're going to need our last five up, but you stay here. We'll manage.'

Sarah nodded imperceptibly and as Sister and Nurse Burton left, Sarah gently turned higher the oxygen; the soft hissing was louder; the water bubbled more rapidly in the glass flow-meter; but the sides of the little green rubber bag fluttered a little more weakly.

Dr Brown altered the tap of the glass drip-connection set in the transfusion apparatus and timed the increased speed of the droplets on his watch. 'Doing anything?'

Sarah's fingers were on the barely perceptible pulse in one cold chubby wrist and her gaze on her watch. She shook her head without looking up.

He glanced from her downcast face to the child's, then stooped and gently touched her forehead and looked into her unseeing eyes. He straightened his tired back, hunched his tired narrow shoulders and stared down, and his dark eyes were sad, defeated and angry. 'Someone must've been with her,' he muttered, thinking aloud. And Sarah, recognizing this, didn't answer. Whenever deeply moved she was habitually silent and it was as obvious to him, as to her and the whole staff, that if some older relative or friend had taken the little girl to the Market, since no one had yet come searching for her, either that person was still searching elsewhere, or was an UNKNOWN admission in this or some other hospital, or still buried alive, or dead.

Dr Brown stepped slightly back from the bed, still staring down, his hands hanging limply at his sides, and stethoscope hanging limply from his neck. 'I must get back to Casualty. Nothing I can do here – but if you want me, anytime, anything – shout.'

Sarah didn't look up. 'Thank you, doctor.'

'For bloody what, Sarah?' he spat under his breath.

She looked up momentarily and straight into his eyes. She said very quietly, firmly, 'Skip the breast-beating, Paddy. You didn't drop it and you're not God.'

He flushed deeply. His quick brain forced the recognition that he had needed the mental slap in the face but he resented passionately that she should have recognised and administered this. He was a conscientious young doctor, but even although sufficiently experienced to realise that there were times when the bedside had to be left to the nurses as good nursing could give the only possible help, he was not yet old enough to accept this situation with equanimity. Suddenly he resented just as passionately Sarah's skilled, silent presence and had to soothe his resentment by writing-off her silence as callousness.

He backed out slowly, then turned, and swept from the ward and into the flat, mentally cursing that cold bitch Sarah Thane, the war he had repeatedly insisted was none of his bloody business, the damned fools that had let that poor sweet-faced baby of a child back to London, London for letting itself be turned into mincemeat, the damned British Government for its impotence to defend its citizens from the damned rockets, the damned minds of the damned men that made the rockets, and the whole damned Medical Profession for being as much good as a damned sick headache when it came to saving unsaveable lives. . . . Then, as he swept by the open bathroom door the sight of Val Martin's pretty, concerned, profile, and hand stroking the untidy head of the woman weeping in her arms, cut off his cursing. That was how a nurse – a woman – should be, he thought, and remembered the tears he had seen in her eyes when she slid out the canvas. A girl like her would love kids – so did he – no better patients in this world and, Mother of God – in another hour or maybe the two or maybe the less – there would be one less sweet-faced baby of a darling in this damned hideous world.

He walked on, very slowly, back to Casualty, his hands in his trouser pockets, head lowered and wet eyes fixed on the floor ahead.

CHAPTER FOUR

IT was a quarter-to-ten when Charles and Paddy Brown left the dining-room together. Paddy had on a clean white coat and had rinsed the dust from his hair and the long forelock slanting to his right eyebrow was no blacker than the shadows under his eyes. He went into Henry Ward, leaving Charles to limp on to Central Hall where he leant against one of the empty pedestals to light a cigarette before going over to Paddy's room in the Doctors' House. 'All yours, Charlie. Bunks in the tombs for all stooges of residents this damned night and no takers on our chances of getting to 'em.' Paddy stifled a yawn. 'You'll find a half of gin lying around somewhere. Help yourself.'

Charles didn't want a drink. All he wanted was a bath, a bed, and the energy to get over the road. His left leg felt on fire and he was so dogtired it took his thumb three flicks to light his lighter. He had just snapped it out when he saw Sarah Thane coming down the corridor and walking like an exhausted old woman with her folder cloak over one arm. Then she stopped, slung the cloak over her shoulders and went out onto the terrace by the only corridor FIRE EXIT door visible from his position.

For perhaps another two minutes he stayed against the pedestal, smoking, and looking at that door as if it was the first he had ever seen. Then he pushed himself upright, limped painfully back to the corridor, stubbed out his cigarette amongst the other fag-ends and ash in a sand-bucket and went out by the same door. Once outside, he had to lean against it until his eyes grew acclimatised to the initially impenetrable darkness of the blacked-out city on a moonless, overcast night.

That night was warm for late February, but refreshingly cool after the stuffy warmth of the dining-room and steamy tropical heat of the theatre. The Thames was at high water. The incoming tide had brought in a breeze just strong enough to have cleared from the immediate vicinity of the hospital most of the huge dust cloud that had hovered over the south bank all afternoon. The breeze hadn't the power to move the heavy, low clouds pressing down over London and that roughly one mile behind him were tinted pink by the reflected rays of the rescue squads arc lamps. That pink in the sky would be there all night and all tomorrow night even although already the victims being dug out alive had been reduced to about 5 per cent and the bodies of the dead had become increasingly harder to identify as individual human bodies.

The lazily moving air on his face smelt strongly of salt, tar and traffic exhaust and only faintly of the dust still clinging to the back of his nostrils and throat. Anaesthetic fumes still clung to his hair, though he had held his head under a cold tap in the surgeons' changing room after the SSO's, 'Right! All walking-wounded out. Thanks, old chap — sorry, forgotten your name — we can cope now. Up to full strength as Profs. and pundits are back from the Hut. Get along to the dining-room and grab some supper before you push off.'

Slowly, the black curtain was breaking up and forming shadowy shades, patches of charcoal-black, purple-black and far ahead and on both far sides was pierced by moving pinpoints of light made by the traffic crawling behind slits in blackened headlamps along the opposite embankment and the invisible, nearest bridges. On either of his near sides, the solid, jutting-forward shadows of Blocks 4 and 5 loomed up like sheer cliffs. Further away the stone-flagged

70

inlet of the terrace that divided them darkened to a bottomless black cavern, and, in contrast, lightened to charcoal the broad sweep of the terrace beyond that was edged by a sturdy stone parapet that hid from him the embankment below the river. But he could now depict clearly the petrified black lace outlines of the Houses of Parliament, Big Ben seeming a shadowy Cleopatra's needle in the wrong place, and the jagged outlines and gaps dotting the length of the far bank. And he noticed academically, as he had in other places, how the black-out softened the ugly lines of bombed buildings and laid soothing purple-black carpets over flattened bombsites.

He looked up and down the far bank, up and down, up and down, with the war-conditioned impersonality of a sensitive young man who had seen so much war-destruction and death that his sensitivities here had been hammered numb. But not his war-conditioned reflexes. The sudden wail of a tram turning off a bridge to run down the road passing the hospital – that was now again open to all traffic – was so similar to the scream of a dive-bombing Stuka, that from long forgotten habit his head jerked up and he scanned the quiet, low-sky, heavy with clouds and long-cabled, invisible balloons.

He limped onto the terrace and stopped to quarter its length for the white glimmers of a cap and apron skirt beneath a long, navy cloak. No sign. He moved to the parapet and briefly glanced down at the black river and the gently bobbing, flatly oblonged shadows of an anchored line of empty coal barges. The water slapping their sides made the sound of tearing silk and in the blackness under the invisible bridge on the right, the suddenly struck match of an invisible river policeman on the deck of his unseen boat flared like a Very light.

He turned his back on the river and leant against the parapet to light another cigarette and think things over. He didn't think she had spotted him just now, but he

71

could be wrong and she could have made the getaway to avoid him. Or just to avoid the whole human race? If that last, he knew the feeling. Time after time he'd needed privacy and solitude as a man dying of thirst needs water. Yet, if for either reason, what right had he to chase after her? David's old pal? Stuff that. Paddy had known David pretty well but just now at supper Paddy had said she'd never mentioned her brother to him, nor he to her. Paddy had talked one hell of a lot at supper. He always had, specifically when steamed-up, and tonight the lid had blown off. Shaken rigid by today's show — and who wasn't? Words were Paddy's safety-valve, but not everyone's, he had reflected whilst listening to Paddy and saying very little. Paddy hadn't noticed, or changed. He had always been able to listen to patients and pundits, but otherwise all he heard was his own voice. ' . . . lay you a year's pay, Charlie, she never turned a hair when she turned off the oxygen — just bloody routine. What's it to her that poor baby of a child was the fifteenth we've had croak [die] in the one bloody afternoon — not to mention the seven BIDs [Brought In Dead]. Only one in Alex and just before prayers so they weren't delayed. Perish the bloody thought anything should delay ward routine! What if our morgue fridges are packed like sardine tins! Did you hear it's now sixty-two stiffs on the site?' Charles had nodded. 'Mother of God, Charlie, I've had this bloody war — when's it going to end?' Charles had shrugged. 'Why should I worry? None of my bloody business. Want coffee? I'll get the two. Black, is it? Coming up.'

Where the hell had she got to? He had been sure she would be leaning against the parapet somewhere. All the day nurses came on at seven-thirty in the morning, she had been on her feet over fifteen hours and if still out there would have to lean against something as there was damn-all to sit upon — As you were! Young Harry's steps — if they hadn't had it.

72

He limped more quickly on past Block 5, the burnt-out shell of Block 6 and into the next flagged inlet that was flanked at the left by the vast mound of the rubble of Block 7. In the centre of that inlet and to face the river, the Victorians had erected a statue of King Henry VI to mark the four hundredth anniversary of his granting a charter to the monastic Hospice of St Martha. In reality the charter had been granted by the Regent when the king was six years old, but the Victorian sculptor had depicted him in young manhood and modelled the Plantagenet bonnet, face and piously folded long-fingered hands from an ancient portrait of Henry VI at around that age. The slightly larger-than-lifesize stone figure stood on a four-foot-square polished granite plinth surrounded by three wide, shallow granite steps that on fine days in peacetime had been as thronged with seated medical students as Trafalgar Square with strolling pigeons.

It was very dark between mound and shell. He had to stop and flick on and hold up his lighter. Then he saw Sarah and the statue flat on its back a few feet from where he stood. He pinched out the flame and breathed as if he had been running. She had neither seen nor heard him. She sat hunched on the top step, her back to the front of the plinth, her face buried in the navy cloak that covered her upraised knees and whole small body. He had glimpsed her shaking shoulders, but he didn't hear her quiet weeping until he was within touching distance, and still she didn't seem to hear him. He steadied himself with one hand on the plinth and before touching her said evenly, 'It's Charles Bradley, Sarah,' and before either was properly aware of it had lowered himself to sit by her, put one arm round her and drawn her against his shoulder. After that he neither moved nor spoke until she gave the long shuddering sigh that ends weeping. He used his free hand to light two cigarettes simultaneously, kept one between his lips and, guided by his little finger, felt for her lips and put the other cigarette to them. 'If you don't smoke, spit it out,' he said.

'I do. Thanks.' She sighed again, but more calmly. 'Sorry — '

'Scrub that.' He lightly touched the hand she was using to dry her ravaged face. 'Very cold.'

'Not very. Bit.'

'Right.' He drew her closer and folded both arms around her. 'Any better?'

'Yes, thanks,' muttered Sarah. She was too physically and emotionally exhausted to recall, much less be troubled by, trivialities such as embarrassment and conventional attitudes, or the fact that if her nursing authorities could now see her smoking in uniform in a man's arms on hospital territory she would be thrown out of Martha's in the next half-hour without any hope of a testimonial or Martha's Training School badge. That she was totally unsurprised by this situation only surprised her vaguely until, like a memory from the distant past, she slowly recalled how, in the few minutes of their first meeting this afternoon, she had seen Charles Bradley with that peculiar clarity that only comes at first meetings. This is what he'd do, she thought, and then smelling the anaesthetic on his hair — yes, that's what he would've done. She finished the cigarette before asking, 'Come out for air too, Charles?'

He had earlier wondered how he would answer this kind of question from her, then characteristically shelved the problem to be dealt with when necessary. The problem had ceased to exist from the moment he took her into his arms. 'No. I saw you coming out from Central Hall and came after.'

She moved her head to look up at him in the darkness and the ruined bow at the back of her cap brushed his chin. 'Thanks a lot.'

'That's all right. Another fag?'

'No, thanks. You have one.'

'Not now.' He eased them higher against the plinth then

locked his hands together at her waist. 'Handy backrest.'

'Hard on your back.'

'It'll survive.'

Sarah made no comment and Charles cursed himself for a tactless fool and slightly tightened his hold to comfort her and himself. He knew precisely why he had had to come after her and that, whatever the turn-up, this afternoon she had come into his life with the explosive power of a V2. He had heard and read of this happening, but never before believed it could be true, but she seemed to have suddenly released some secret resources within him that had been awaiting their meeting to enrich his understanding and his whole life.

At last, Sarah said, 'Forty-four patients in Alex when I came off. Two empty beds left. One wasn't – ' her voice cracked 'a little girl – UNKNOWN – no one came for her – I expect no one was left to come and – and – '

'I heard. I know. You were with her.'

'Yes,' she said, and again for some time they were silent. She broke the silence. 'When this war's over and they put up Memorials, they should put up one to THE UNKNOWN CIVVY WOMAN and THE UNKNOWN CHILD.' She paused. 'I don't expect they will.'

'I'm afraid not, but they bloody should.'

They fell silent thinking of Alex and the hospital now, and that silence lasted a very long time and as it continued grew more empathetic with every passing minute. The surrounding darkness didn't deepen; on nights such as this, once twilight ended it became and remained dark as midnight. The breeze dropped; the drone of the traffic and wails of the trams were a little louder; but neither noticed. They didn't hear the lapping of the river or even Big Ben marking each quarter–hour. Neither could bear to talk more of all that had happened today and that they knew they would never be able to forget. One day, perhaps, they would talk of it again together. One day, perhaps.

Eventually, reluctantly, Sarah asked, 'What time is it?'

'Hold it.' He flicked the lighter on over his watch-face. 'Twenty to eleven.'

'Oh God. I must get back. Our Home's locked at eleven. I haven't a key or late leave and if I have to ring to get in I'll have to explain to Home Sister why it's taken me nearly one hour and a half or whatever to cross the road.' She disentangled herself without difficulty and stood up. 'Thanks a lot.'

'Thank you.' He hauled himself up on the plinth, blindly. 'When did young Harry buy it?'

'Must've been this afternoon's blast. He was back up yesterday.' She groped for his arm. 'Watch out for him.'

'I will.' He caught and held onto her small hand. 'Long way round to the road from here still open? Paddy Brown's loaned me his room.'

'Good and yes, it is – oh, heck!' She stubbed her foot on the prone statue. 'Sorry, Harry.'

'He can take it.' He lit his lighter and they stooped to peer at the cracked but otherwise intact figure, bonnet and stone face. 'Say that again. Harry was down when I left.'

'He's always going for a Burton. The doodle that flattened the remains of 8 last month had him down again and Dacey again press-ganging the JCOs and Cas. dressers into bunging him back up.'

'As also before I left.'

Sarah nodded, forgetting the lighter was out and it was too dark for him to see her response until she felt the tightening of his comforting hand. He's kind and he's sweet, she thought wearily, and that doodle's worried him and he'd had and done enough. 'That was the only doodle-bug we had on Martha's, all it did was bring down Harry and a few bottles and test-tubes off a few shelves in Cas. and the In-Patients' Lab. and I don't remember hearing one since. Jerry must've run out. Anyway, I expect Dacey and the boys'll have Harry back up tomorrow.'

'Good. Let's go.'

They walked away hand-in-hand and carefully in the darkness and too tired, saddened and grateful for each other's presence to suspect that what Sarah had just said was both right and wrong.

MARCH, 1945

CHAPTER FIVE

'DACEY here, Nurse Thane. And how's Alex doing?'

'Couldn't be quieter, thanks,' said Sarah, knowing Dacey knew this, and automatically tapping the telephone's wooden shelf and watching the peaceful half-empty ward in which two visitors were sitting chatting quietly by every occupied bed and Nurse Burton, tall, striking and starched, was presiding over the 'second cups for patients and visitors' tea-trolley with her habitual air of the duchess she would undoubtedly become if her very sexual mouth succeeded in overcoming her current, openly expressed determination to be a future President of the Royal College of Nursing for England and Wales. The back of Sarah's mind registered 'my money's on the duke'; and the forefront, 'Dacey's got some private gen for me'. And then, as Val's fiancé's welfare was presently on the minds of all Val's friends, Sarah glanced at Paddy Brown. He was draped against the opposite flat wall covertly watching Val through the open dutyroom doorway whilst telling four of the latest batch of medical students about penicillin's revolutionary effects on the course and treatment of acute pneumonia. ' . . . don't expect you chaps will ever see one go through to the old ninth-day crisis when either the temp. suddenly soared fatally, or dropped dramatically from – say – 106 plus to just above or below normal, that fall known as "by crisis", or less dramatically, and jerkily, with every peak always lower than the last, termed "by lysis". . . . '

Sarah said into the receiver, 'How goes Cas., Dacey?'

Paddy glanced at her without losing the thread of his discourse, then returned his covert gaze to Val Martin sitting facing Nurse Yates across the clean-sheet-covered dutyroom table stacked with new-made packs of clean dressings. Val was cutting eight-inch squares from layers of fresh gauze and Nurse Yates was folding them into packs to fill the last in the row of dressing drums on the long mahogany shelf against the wall behind them that were awaiting collection for sterilisation by the Surgical Stores porter on his six o'clock evening round.

Dacey said, 'Can't bind, nurse. Not the one customer. So I thought I'd give you a tinkle with the nice bit of gen I just had from Captain Bradley. Seems that doodlebug that come down lunchtime today got Fulham, not Acton like we heard, and done no worse than cause a few splinters. Come down on another old bombsite, it did, flattened it nicely, and Captain Bradley says the cops told him not the one serious casualty as all gone flat nicely. Well, had the practice.'

'Great!' smiled Sarah, restraining her curiosity over why Charles should be in Cas. in the certainty that it was about to be assuaged. Dacey was unarguably the best-informed source of war, hospital and inter-staff-relationships news in Martha's.

'As I said to Captain Bradley, nurse! Just stepped back, he had, for something he'd forgotten up the In-Patients' Lab., he said. Still, mustn't keep you. Don't take any wooden tanners (sixpences), nurse.' He rang off, smiling to himself and settling more comfortably on the high stool at the half-open stable-door of the head porter's lodge. It was Saturday afternoon, Sister Casualty's alternative free weekend off, Casualty Hall was empty of patients and the mid-March sun was slanting in through the gap between, and over the tops of, the blast and sandbag walls. The afternoon two-to-four Visiting Time was nearly over and the visitors in their war-shabby civilian clothes and war-worn uniforms were beginning to trail out, freed of the flowers and fruit they had brought in and telling each other he, or she, looked more than a mite better and wasn't it wonderful what hospitals could do for you these days and a proper treat to see a bit of sun and the daffodils coming up lovely in the parks for all today was only St Patrick's Day and spring official like still round the corner.

It was the third weekend after the Tuesday that inter-hospital had been labelled M-Day. On the following Tuesday the local street-market had re-opened on a neigh-bouring bombsite granted a special licence by the London County Council; at the close of that day, when the licensed – and unlicensed – stall-holders had totted up, their takings were the highest since the outbreak of the war.

In Martha's, M-Day had long vanished into old hospital history. On Wednesday and Thursday of that week, long, extra convoys of ambulances and ambulance coaches had gone down to the Hut and the Large Emergency Medical Services' hospital from which Nurse Burton had recently been transferred. By Wednesday night all the wards' emergency beds had been returned to their flats' store-rooms; by Thursday, the 'start the night with ten empty beds' order had been reinstated, the bodies and possessions of the identified dead handed over to their relatives and those of the unidentified, which included the body of the little girl that had died in Alex, to the civic authorities. The official figures of that rocket's victims, were total known dead: 101; seriously injured, 128; as ever, the number of minor injured was not given. Martha's was just one of the hospitals south of the river that had treated the ignored category; Casualty treated and then sent home 314.

In war, as in peace, tragedy was a routine hospital occurrence that in the event had to be accepted, and afterwards, if only outwardly, forgotten. For some forget-fulness came more easily than for others, but even the most retentive memories found a form of amnesia in the near non-stop battle with the clock and continuous variety of wartime hospital life. So much kept happening, kept altering, not merely from day to day but often hour to hour, that frequently yesterday became old history before today was out and last week lost in the distant past.- Seldom, if ever, did any nine-days-wonder last full-term. M-Day lasted until the following Saturday afternoon.

Upon that afternoon another rocket landed in Martha's 'zone', but amongst old war ruins as the flying bomb Dacey had just mentioned. The rocket dug a crater sixty foot deep and eighty wide without causing even one minor human casualty. But its point of impact had been closer to the hospital than the Market, and the standing blocks had been in the direct path of the blast waves and badly shaken. After structural inspection of all three early on Sunday morning, 5 had been deemed unsafe, Henry Ward closed and its entire staff and patients evacuated to the Hut by that evening.

The news that Henry was to be evacuated buzzed around the hospital grapevine before the inspectors had finished their first, verbal, report. Each buzz of the grapevine embroidered upon its predecessor. Not just Henry – the whole hospital! Not just the hospital – London! What could the wretched Government do but evacuate the capital seeing it could do damn-all about the rockets. Whatever the RAF and Yanks were doing from the air and the Allies Armies on the ground in Europe they still hadn't got over the damned Rhine, and some rocket launching-pads somewhere were still in very good order as the miserable things were still dropping like leaves in autumn. (The last was an overstatement; only approximately 232 long-range rockets were launched on London in February.)

March had opened to a slight increase in the rockets and the unexpected – to the average civilian Londoner – return of the flying bombs. But as the V1s, in comparison with

84

last year's onslaughts, came sparsely and were so familiar, with the exceptions of the occasions when one switched off its engine overhead, they tended to be ignored by civilian Londoners, unless they happened to work in the police, ARP, fire and ambulance services or hospitals. None the less, again in comparison with last year, so far this March, Martha's had only admitted a trickle of V1 casualties and treated a few dozen 'minors' in casualty. All the admissions had been fit for transfer to country hospitals within the statutory twenty-four hours, since all were from London.

London had learnt to fear, to abominate and to cope with its doodlebugs and this was, above all, never to look up when one switched off anywhere above and to dive for the nearest safe cover for the head and face. In shops, as elsewhere indoors, staff and customers crouched in unison, heads buried in laps or between knees or under counters or shopping bags if nothing else was handy. If outside and there was no near shop or other doorway, or public shelter to dive into, flat on the face with the arms folded across the back of the head whether upon a wet pavement, station platform, public park, back garden, or any other outdoor locality. All stayed crouched or prone without fail during the few seconds between the bomb's switch-off, dive, and explosion at ground level. The number of seconds varied with individual counting, and was never beyond 15 and generally between 8 and 10.

Charles heard his first flying bomb when in Professor Pathology's window-bricked office at the river end of the In-Patients' Pathological Laboratory. Professor Pathology was a stout man in his late fifties with untidy grey hair, and unless using a microscope, a lighted cigarette in his mouth and an unlit spare tucked above his right ear. He was saying, 'Not a bad idea, Bradley. Potter around in our midst, by all means. Take a bit of blood for us here and there – do the odd blood count – always glad of extra hands and one of the advantages of pathology is that it allows any chap in a long white coat with a box of tricks under his arm to potter around the wards and departments at will. Persona grata, are we – ' he broke off to listen. 'Stone me! Hear what I hear?'

'That faint roaring, sir?'

'More of a chug-chug-chug. You'll hear. Coming this way but I suspect too fast for us. Well, well. Thought we'd done with that nastiness. He must've kept a few back for a rainy day. Is it raining?'

'Not when I came in, sir.' The distant chugging was becoming a jerky growl. 'Flying bomb?'

'Doodlebug or doodle to London, old chap. Elsewhere, buzz-bomb. Very infra dig.' He had to raise his voice. 'Not seen one?'

Charles, looking upwards, shook his head as the bomb roared by above.

The Professor glanced at Charles's ribbons whilst waiting to be audible. 'Restrain your curiosity if one switches off anywhere above when you're outside. They dive at a slant but the slant can be deflected by the wind and other imponderables. Treat the switch-off as you would a shell. The blast's particularly destructive as they explode above ground. We had some very nasty blast injuries last year, specifically in the early weeks when curiosity tended to overcome prudence.' He sliced a flattened hand across his face and nearly knocked the cigarette from his lips. 'Just so.' He stopped to listen. 'Fading. As I thought, too fast for us. Possible Lewisham or New Cross. Nasty. So you've found somewhere in Chelsea?'

'Beaufort Street. Ground Floor flat and a bit dark and overfurnished, but just the job. It belongs to the sister of an RAF chap I was warded with. She decided to move out last year and rent it furnished and as takers seem a bit thin on the ground doesn't object to short leases. Her brother fixed it up for me in a couple of trunk calls. I moved in this last weekend.'

'Whilst poor old Henry hit the DIL and was banished to the sticks, eh? You wasted no time.'

'One of my eight weeks gone tomorrow, sir.'

'True. Chelsea. Yes. Bit far from Sloane Square but handy for the World's End, Beaufort Street.' The Professor was still looking at him but suddenly Charles sensed, without seeing him. 'Presumably you'll take the Tube to Westminster then walk over the river.'

'Or use the buses or trams.'

'A bus'll mean changing at Victoria, as I recall. My youngest boy had digs near the World's End for a spell before the war. Good bus service, he used to say, but if I were you, Bradley, I'd use Tubes as much as possible, pro tem.'

'Point taken, sir. Thanks.'

The Professor stubbed out his cigarette, pulled the one from above his right ear, stuck it in his mouth and before he lit up pushed another above his ear. 'When do you want to start? Straight off? Why not? You'll need a coat – we'll fix you up. Come and meet Dr Anthony. He'll show you the shop.'

'Thanks very much, sir,' said Charles without asking the present whereabouts of the Professor's youngest son, as he could guess the answer too well. Later, he did ask Dr Anthony, 'Bought it?'

'Yes. Killed in action when your lot broke through the Trasimene Line last June. In that show?' Charles nodded impassively. Dr Anthony looked from Charles's face to his 8th Army ribbon. 'That won't have hurt you with the old man. Young Tim hit him even harder than his eldest boy – missing since Singapore – but the old man's an optimistic type and getting blood from a stone's a damned sight easier than getting the names of British prisoners out of the Japanese. Very hard hit over young Tim. Great shame. Very nice youngster.'

'Hellish tough.'

Dr Anthony took another look at Charles's face. 'Yes.'

A few days later, on the first red-letter evening of his sick leave, sitting with Sarah in the front stalls of a theatre in Shaftsbury Avenue, Charles heard a flying bomb switch off directly overhead. When first he heard it approaching, he looked sideways at Sarah and saw that, as the entire sparse audience, she had stiffened to listen for it, without removing her gaze from the stage. The play was a domestic comedy of which he had never heard and Sarah said had had enthusiastic reviews, but, as all London theatres, was getting poor houses owing to the combination of the continuing fighting in North Western Europe and air attacks on London.

They had met that lunchtime, not by chance as Sarah assumed, for the first time since M-Day night, and she had astonished and delighted him by saying she was off that evening, had just collected from Matron's office two free tickets for a play she particularly wanted to see, that none of her set were off to go with her and would he like to do so.

'Very much, thanks, but I shouldn't use – '

'Phooey!' Her lovely eyes laughed up at him. 'No buts! You're eligible for our free tickets. Every member of the staff is eligible and you're an acting, unpaid, supernumerary pathologist – or has the grapevine got it wrong again and the Army's just taken over the In-Patients' Lab?' He shook his head smiling and marvelling at how enchanting she looked when she smiled. 'Bang on! The London theatre managers are wonderful to us and inundate Matron's office with free tickets always for the best seats. Val Martin and another of my set saw the show last evening – had them laughing like drains, they said. And luckily, today they've a matinée, so the evening show doesn't begin till six-thirty. I'll have half-an-hour to get changed and meet you there.' She gave him the tickets. 'Hang onto these.'

'Can't I call for you in a taxi? I'll have time to get one.'

'If you can get one in the rush-hour we'll spend most of

88

the first act in jams.' She hesitated to remind him of his limp, and then realised that, as she, he would always prefer the truth. Not necessarily like. Prefer. 'Look, Charles, I'm not off till six. It'll take me five minutes to get over the road, five to change and in twenty I can make it at the double on foot, as I know all the short cuts. Okay?'

'Very much so, thanks. Meet you in the foyer.'

The bomb was very near, very loud, but the only member of the audience not watching the stage was Charles watching Sarah and concealing his throttling anxiety for her with conscious control. The cast only showed their awareness of what was approaching by raising their voices to full power. Suddenly, the roaring stopped. Charles hauled Sarah sideways and face down into his lap and crouched over her whilst the rest of the audience buried their own faces between their knees and folded their arms over the backs of their heads as none had room or time to lie flat. The stage was suddenly silent, but Charles didn't see what the cast were doing until the thunder of the close explosion faded and with one movement, he, Sarah, and the others in the audience breathlessly sat upright in their seats. The characters on stage were back on their feet, and breathing out. It so chanced that the next line was a remark from the hero to his 'best friend'. 'How you can tolerate this quiet existence, I cannot conceive.' He got no further than, 'How you can tolerate this quiet — ' when his voice was drowned by the audience's shout of laughter that infected all on stage and for the next few minutes the play was held up until the cast, too, could stop laughing. Then the play went on; when it ended, and the thin, appreciative audience insisted upon eight curtain calls, Charles and Sarah were close enough to see that, behind the professional smiles and make up, the entire cast was in tears.

'Sarah sighed happily, 'Good, as I hoped. What did you think?'

'Better.'

She was glad he had enjoyed it and that she had obeyed the impulse to ask him to accompany her when she had run into him when she had been coming from first lunch and he about to go into second. Neither she nor the grapevine were aware of Charles's new habit of keeping a watch on the to-ing and fro-ing from the dining-room during the nurses' luncheon periods, as he was long experienced in the use of protective cover. But he had been in her mind from that night on the terrace, as his behaviour then was all she could yet bear to recall of M-Day. Later, on his first morning in the In-Patients' Lab, she had heard from the grapevine that he had rented a Chelsea flat for his leave and intended spending most of it brushing up on pathology as so much pathology work can be done seated. She had been disturbingly reminded that had she and not David been killed, he too would have had no one to come back to. Two world wars had decimated or demolished so many of two generations of British families. Her father had been the only one of his parents' four sons to survive the first; her mother, whom she couldn't remember and who had died of puerperal sepsis after the still-born birth of her third child, had lost both brothers in the Great War. None of the uncles Sarah had only known as fading photographs of young men in uniform had been old enough to marry, so she had no first cousins. This had never troubled her, or her brother and she doubted it had Charles, as one didn't miss what one had never had. But she was troubled about Charles's solitary state, as she sensed intuitively that the self-containment it had bred in him had left him singularly undemanding and wary of treading until sure of his ground.

The staff up here is like a stage-crowd, she had thought. Same faces popping up everywhere; few enough for everyone to know every face, who's got an eye on whom, who's playing the field, who's faithful to an absent beloved – and his or her name and vague whereabouts, and who belongs in which tight little social clique. A man of Paddy Brown's temperament would just panzer his way in regardless, and generally get away with it. Paddy's a born good party man. Charles isn't. He would have to be asked to the party and convinced the invitation was genuine before he'd accept it. So she had broken a life-long habit when she obeyed that impulse at lunchtime today.

She was rather glad that she had for her own sake. It had been pleasant to discover they laughed at the same things, though a bit disturbing also to discover that in danger his first thought had been for her and not his own protection. Nursing and the war had taught her that self-preservation was the most powerful of all the primitive instincts and most difficult to disregard. He's not just sweet and kind, he's a good type, and I like him a lot, she thought now with a certainty that surprised her disturbed her still more. It usually took her much longer to make up her mind about people. Why the spot decision on him, she wondered, at first absently and then, when he took her out to supper after the play, with growing concern over the fact that she already liked him too much for peace of mind.

The only man she had loved as a man and not a brother had been an RNVR Lieut. -Commander whom she had first met as a patient in her second year. Their personal relationship had begun after his discharge from hospital, but even so could have cost her job had news of it reached the grapevine. It was an old Martha's maxim that the quickest way to be thrown out for a nurse — short of deliberately poisoning a patient — was to have an affair with one. Only her set had known, and kept the secret. They had similarly supported her a year later when his corvette went down in the Atlantic and he had not been amongst the few survivors fished up by his ship's chummy ship. His death, coming eleven months after her brother's, had devastated Sarah. For months after, she had only felt alive on-duty where she had to forget private grief; off-duty she had seemed to exist only in a grey limbo.

It was like swimming under water, she recollected during that supper after the play; eyes smarting, lungs bursting and always knowing somewhere above was a surface and that sometime one would have to go up for air but daren't yet. Eventually, she had surfaced, outwardly unchanged and inwardly determined – never again for the duration.

I mustn't like him too much, she thought, watching his pleasantly plain, strong face and the expression at the back of the steady grey eyes watching her so incessantly. He's only got eight weeks, this is the second, then he'll have to go. I can't go through all that pain again. I've lost my nerve. I'm a coward, period. But, luckily, though he seems to have taken a bit of a shine to me, he knows the score. He knows that the war giveth these breaks and the war taketh away – and the operative words in this context are 'taketh away'. Only the dumb rush into things in wartime – like Val's John proposing at first date. Crazy! Maybe Val's John isn't so like Paddy as I've been imagining. Paddy can be crazy, but never in a crazy way and Charles is anything but crazy, she thought, over supper and in their taxi back to the Home. Not one pass. Just smoking like a chimney and keeping his hands in his pockets or folded under his arms.

At a few minutes to twelve the taxi drew up at the darkened front steps of the locked Nurses' Home. Sarah had asked Home Sister for a front door key and late-leave that ended at midnight. Any extension beyond that had to be personally requested of Matron and, with very rare exceptions, was only granted to nurses on the night before their weekly day off.

Charles kept the taxi waiting whilst he saw her up the steps and even although every bone he possessed ached with the desire to take her small soft body back into his arms, and to kiss her, he only shook her hand. Since they left the theatre he had sensed she was mentally keeping him at arm's length, but this had neither dimmed the red letter aspect of the occasion for him, nor surprised him. He had little personal conceit, had long been conditioned by current social conventions, and, as Sarah had guessed, was acutely aware that in seven weeks he would have to leave her. He recognised that an unwanted pass now would wreck his hopes of persuading her to spend more of her meagre, precious free time with him, and that the exceptional circumstances that had followed him to hold her in his arms on the terrace had simultaneously made their relationship much easier and much more difficult, especially for him. He was sufficiently in love, and honest, to admit to himself that she no more than liked him. Liking was good enough, pro tem., he thought, thanking her and adding, 'Can we do something like this again, please?'

The handshake reassured her. He knew the score. 'Sure. Thanks again for supper. See you around.'

'Good.'

He waited until the front door closed behind her then limped down the steps and back into the taxi as Big Ben struck midnight.

Sarah passed on to the staff in the flat and dutyroom Dacey's gen on Fulham's latest doodle, but for reasons of her own that included the speed and distorting powers of the hospital grapevine, not how Dacey had come by it. None questioned her on this, since, from her move from Casualty where she and Dacey had become great friends, Dacey's habit of ringing her and with odd bits of gen in quiet moments, when their respective Sisters were off-duty, was as well-known as Dacey's universal omniscience. Paddy Brown said there was no doubt in his mind Fulham must be full of the Irish and St Patrick had been on the job, which made Val smile and him forget he had not yet forgiven Sarah Thane for whatever it was she had done to annoy him. It was his pride that he never forgot an insult — when he remembered it.

Sarah returned smiling to the desk to be visibly available to any visitor who wanted a private talk with the nurse-in-charge. It was Sister Alex's alternate free weekend, but she was spending it in the Home and at her own instigation had arranged for Sarah to be free to leave hospital territory for the evening when she went off-duty at six and Val took over Alex until the night staff came on at nine. Heaven bless Sister, thought Sarah, looking round the peaceful ward that Val would run admirably providing there was no flap. Then, very briefly, Sarah thought — how like Charles to come back over two hours early to make sure he doesn't have to keep me waiting two minutes and how — how lovely! She quenched the thought swiftly and exchanged smiles with Miss Evers.

Miss Evers, still in 36, was now the only Alex patient who had been in on M-Day, and had been kept bedridden in London by a right femoral thrombosis she had developed on her eleventh post-operative day. Once more, the majority of her fellow-patients were surgical and only those in 1 and 2 medical. Both of these had been admitted a few days ago within hours of each other with acute lobar pneumonia. Owing to their penicillin courses they were making uneventful recoveries at a speed that would have been medically impossible up to the late spring of last year.

Mrs Hicks had died in her sleep one night in the week before last; and for the last three weeks Noreen had been warded in the Hut. The rocket on the Market had finally persuaded her mother to consent to the transfer and to take unpaid leave-of-absence from her job and move down to the nearest village to the Hut as the bed, breakfast and supper guest of one of the small army of Women's Voluntary Services members in the neighbourhood that had willingly volunteered their homes for this purpose. Lunch, tea, and innumerable odd cups of tea, in London and the Hut,

Martha's traditionally provided freely to all next-of-kin of DILs, and more occasionally when, as here, there was genuine need to help SILs (Seriously Ill List patients). That this situation seldom caused any embarrassment was partially due to the fact that Martha's was a great well-endowed voluntary hospital, and partially to the uniformly accepted attitude that amongst nursing and medical staff, patients, relatives and other visitors, 'money' was a forbidden topic. It was obvious to all that from the hours the whole staff worked – with even staff nurses earning £60 per year and registrars, £208, that none had chosen their professions for its financial return and that fundamentally the hospital existed for one reason, to do good to the human race. Not that this reason was ever mentioned, but its existence founded the atmosphere of the whole scattered hospital and was itself the foundation of the strong nurse-patient, doctor-patient bonds that over and over, for generations were born in every ward. 'The poor young nurses – lovely girls – not right the way they have to work . . .' 'The poor young doctors – lovely young gentlemen – not right the way they have to work. . . .' still said the patients as their predecessors had for generations.

Paddy finished his dissertation, dismissed the students with an airy wave, and strolled over to lean against one lintel of the open dutyroom doorway and join in the stock-makers' quiet conversation. It was Dr Roberts's alternate free 'weekend' from lunchtime today until tomorrow night's rounds, so Paddy was acting-SMO. The whole hospital was quiet, Casualty knew he was in Alex, and seeing the way the cards were dealt, he, personally, couldn't think of a better place to be at this moment. He said reflectively, 'This scene reminds me of the Hut in May last year. In every dutyroom you nurses were making stock by the ton whilst in every ward beds were being emptied like patients were going out of fashion.'

The nurses had just been discussing the US 9th Army's capture of Remagen bridge over the Rhine ten days ago and Nurse Yates had taken vast umbrage with the British Army for letting the Yanks across first. With rare tact she had kept it to herself, as Martin was already half round the bend over not having had a letter from her flipping POW fiancé since Christmas. So that to say what she thought about Monty would probably send her clean round the bend and she, Nurse Yates, had to work under her this evening – but at least Grey (the senior third year) would be back at five and though she looked like the back of a bus and was thirty when she started, old Grey knew her stuff.

Val answered Paddy's remark with a vague smile. Nurse Yates, being never backward in coming forward, responded firmly, 'It was just so obvious the Second Front was about to start any minute, Dr Brown. Obvious from the minute the Hut began emptying. I don't know why people bother to have spies in wartime. Only got to hang around hospitals to know what's about to happen. Soon as big battles are expected wards start emptying and nurses making mountains of stock. We were all sure the Hut would fill with Second Front casualties – instead we filled with London's doodle casualties,' she added in a tone that echoed the umbrage this had caused her.

He heard the umbrage and his dark eyes smiled into Val's pretty, trusting, pale blue ones. She blushed faintly and looked quickly down at her busy hands. Damn the worthy John, he thought, and said tritely as his mind was elsewhere, 'You pays your money and you takes your choice, Nurse Yates.'

She was indignant. 'The Hut didn't pick what it got, doctor. Just got it.'

'Like pal Jerry.' He looked in a different way at Val's downcast, ethereal face and thought aloud, 'Remember the sky over the Hut on those May evenings?'

Nurse Yates didn't, but Val did, so she had to look up at

him for comfort and their eyes shared the silent memories. Memories of long, lovely, twilight country evenings scented by the pines on the surrounding hills and higher above the hillside upon which sprawled the improvised hospital, and by the fragrance of the wallflowers blooming in wooden tubs on either side of every wooden and nissen hut entrance and the main gates that opened into a steep, high-banked, winding lane. And high above, the wide country sky totally covered by black umbrellas of bombers in formation, flying eastwards. Umbrella followed umbrella; one moved on, another appeared; lovely evening after lovely evening, flying east in unbroken formation. Then, night after night in the small hours, the droning above returned, on and on, but now moving westwards, but the droning was thinner, often much thinner; and, as often, much later, came the sounds that caught the breath, tightened the throat and were made by solitary, wounded aircraft desperately trying to stay airborne and reach the first home base.

Val had dreaded those black umbrellas for the crews that flew them, for what their bombs must do, for what those bombs might have to do, unwittingly, to the prisoner-of-war camps in Germany and upon German-occupied territory. And still going on, she thought – still!

Paddy read the thought in her widened eyes and said quickly, 'One thing's sure, nurse. Jerry'll do his best to safeguard his POWs. He's going to want them for swops.'

'You honestly think so?'

'Cross my heart and hope to die. Jerry's no mug. He knows better than most the meaning of quid pro quo – hence no poison gas this time round and all our civvy gasmasks gathering dust. He's always known damn well that if he dropped a few canisters on British cities the RAF would do likewise on his before he'd got out his next Sieg Heil!' He clicked his heels and outstretched his right arm in the Nazi salute. 'And if that doesn't get this enemy alien up against a wall nothing will!'

Val laughed quietly, gratefully – then had to tell herself there was no disloyalty to John in her gratitude for Paddy Brown's attempts to amuse her. Anyway, Paddy was always making people laugh – he was that type.

Nurse Yates was not amused. 'You may be an alien, Dr Brown, but surely not an enemy alien?'

'Just a simple fifth columnist, nurse.'

'You must be joking!'

'I? Perish the thought! No more sober man in Martha's and may I be struck down if I – Mother of God! He heard me!' He scowled upwards at the sudden distant but fast approaching chug-chug-chugging. 'When are the RAF and coastal ack-ack bods going to get off their backsides? Here's another they've let slip through – ' his voice was stopped not by the much louder jerky roar but by the bomb's explosion in mid-air. 'Blown itself up! That settles it, girls.' He leant against the lintel mournfully. 'Move over St Patrick. I've had it. There's no doubt at all – God must be an Englishman.'

Even Nurse Yates laughed.

'The bits dropped into the river just in front of County Hall.'

Sarah, briefly jolted back to reality, demanded, 'You didn't watch it, Charles?'

He shook his head, smiling and thinking how sweet was her concern and how enchantingly her deep purple blouse accentuated the pearly softness of her throat and the colour of her eyes. 'Lady, I values my neck. Dacey told me when I was hanging around for the taxi he'd laid on.'

She smiled and contentedly slid back into the dream-world that continued to enfold her, though the theatre lights were on for the interval. He watched her in a companionable silence and let his pleasure in her presence temporarily exclude from his thoughts all those vital personal problems that were presently insoluble. He also avoided thinking about the item of war gen he had unexpectedly collected when slipping out to the bar for a packet of cigarettes. He had run into a man with whom he had once served months and last met in a Cairo bar in the winter of 1942. After the usual exchanges, 'Heard the latest balls-up, Charles?'

'Which one?'

'Remagen bridge. Bloody thing must've thought it was London bridge. Fell into the Rhine today. Back to square one . . .'

Not for Sarah now, thought Charles returning to his seat. War was off-limits, tonight.

Her love for the theatre, the passing of all her training examinations and concomitant removal of the need to attend and write-up lectures and study in her free time, had, thanks to London's theatre managers, resulted in her now having seen nearly every play currently on in the West End, at least once. But earlier this week, when he had heard she was off this evening and suggested a date, as he had reluctantly foreseen, she had had to turn it down. 'Sorry. Sister's weekend off and I shouldn't be too far from Alex. Can I take a raincheck?'

'Anytime.'

Then, in her lunch half-hour today, from one of the public boxes in Casualty Hall, she had rung the number of his flat's telephone that he had given her with the address and a carefully casual, 'You must see it, sometime.' That she had echoed 'Sometime,' and changed the subject hadn't surprised him. No etchings for Sarah, he'd thought wrily — and loved her for it.

When she had rung him today her young voice had vibrated with excitement. 'Charles, are you booked else-where for this evening or can I pick up that raincheck and have you seen *Richard III*?'

'No. Yes, please. No.'

99

She laughed. 'Bang on! Mrs Ames has just way-laid me with two tickets for the last house she got from Matron's office this morning before hearing the WAAF chum she was taking has had her forty-eight cancelled. She says she doesn't want to take anyone else and anyway has seen it already – so've I, but never right to the end as both times were in two-to-fives when I was in Cas. and the matinées don't finish till five – and Mrs Ames, may Heaven reward her, says she'll be in the Home to cover Alex for me. How about it?'

'Fine by me,' said Charles, thinking, the understatement of the war. 'But do you really want a third go?'

'Good God, man, do you realise what you're saying? No, of course you don't as you probably don't know it's in the rep. the Old Vic Company are putting on in the New Theatre in St Martin's Lane – they moved over after the Old Vic bought it. They're doing *Uncle Vanya, Peer Gynt, Arms and the Man* and *Richard III*, and I've seen 'em all and they're all marvellous but Laurence Olivier's Richard is more than that! Wait till you see him creeping over the stage like an evil, black velvet spider and his glorious voice makes the hairs stand up on the back of your neck! Just you wait, Charles!'

'I will, Sarah. I will.'

In that interval, she asked, 'Was I shooting a line?'

'No. Repeat no.' Then he had to say, 'You should always wear that colour.'

'Thank you,' she said smiling and as she didn't want to break the spell for either, she did not tell him or let herself recall that her blouse had once been one of her brother's prep school football shirts that war necessity had forced her to save and use.

Charles's heart warmed to her even more for her graceful acceptance of one of his rarely voiced compliments. There were so many he wanted to pay her, so much he wanted to say to her, that in her presence he was having to guard his tongue as closely as his actions. She had never told him that once she had loved a man killed in this war, but by now he had recognised the symptoms and been hurt by them for her, more than for himself. But as he knew that old scars needed time before the final tenderness faded and was also a young man deeply in love, he knew the time of their friendship to the hour.

Four weeks and one morning to go, he thought, as the house lights went down.

CHAPTER SIX

MISS Evers looked and felt several years younger. 'Do you wonder, Daisy?' she whispered, to avoid disturbing her new neighbour in 35. 'Waited on hand and foot all this time. Couldn't say when I last had such a good rest,' she added in unconscious truth, as it had never struck her that this was the first rest of her adult life.

'That's nice,' whispered Daisy, sweeping on behind Miss Evers's pulled out bed the little heaps of dust and blanket fluff clinging to the damp tealeaves she had earlier scattered all over the ward floor for this purpose.

Mrs Ferrers, the new patient in 35, was pretending to be asleep and lecturing herself on her LMF (Lack of Moral Fibre) in not feeling up to a natter with the kindly old bod hard left who seemed to have been in for the duration. Mrs Ferrers lay in a highly propped posture into which she had been lifted by the night nurses when she had been washed and had her bed re-made long before the day nurses arrived on-duty fifteen minutes ago. She was an attractive, buxom woman in her late thirties, whose husband, a peacetime chartered accountant and present major, had been overseas since being posted to the 14th Army in Burma in August, 1940. By then, at her husband's insistence, Mrs Ferrers, with their four small children, had moved from their marital home in Hull to her home village in the Scottish border country. The children were now in boarding-schools in safe areas. As Mrs Ferrers had a strong sense of family duty and a stoic temperament, despite feeling

102

unwell all last week, upon the day before yesterday she had begun the long journey south to represent her husband at his parent's golden wedding aniversary in their home near Godalming on the 23rd March, that was today.

Her train from Scotland, that was due in London just before midnight, arrived five hours late; every carriage, corridor and the guard's van was packed with weary standing and floor-seated passengers. Throughout the journey Mrs Ferrers stoutly insisted to herself that all that ailed her was lack of oxygen and curse pains. Then, in the early morning taxi from King's Cross to Waterloo, she had fainted on the back seat; the driver peered in his mirror, and drove her straight to Martha's. In less than an hour the SSO had removed her perforated appendix and she was warded in Alex.

For most of yesterday she had been too ill and too nauseated by the lingering after-effects of the general anaesthetic to notice her surroundings or even to tell herself to take a grip. She now forced herself to do both and was mildly interested to discover the huge ward was alive with soft-footed, starched figures whisking beds back into place against walls, straightening bed-casters, stacking away neatly every red screen but the one open across the doorway. It was nearly eight in the morning and the end of the one half-hour in the twenty-four when, officially, the day and night staff were on-duty together. Suddenly the screen was removed from the doorway and a hush fell over the – to Mrs Ferrers – obsessively neat ward where every patient was washed and in a new-made bed. All the nurses had vanished, when she heard what she recognised as Big Ben chiming eight and Sister walked in followed by the nurses in single file in order of seniority and then, as if drilled like guardsmen, unfolded the hems of their clean apron skirts, fell upon their knees, lowered their capped heads, and upraised their clasped hands whilst Sister, kneeling at the desk, read the Morning Prayer from the

Book of Common Prayer.

Mrs Ferrers added her murmur to the chorused Lord's Prayer and after the Grace, wondered, am I in a convent or a hospital? She dimly remembered there had been prayers last night. Surely, once was enough? Bit olde-worlde all this — but then so were the nurses' dinkie little Victorian caps with butterfly bows behind and all the lace on Sister's — but hadn't anyone told them this was the twentieth century and, actually, there was a war on? Oh well, face it Isobel, my girl — if you had the luck to have a cushy billet in a reserved occupation — nice work if you could get it. . . .

Always, immediately after prayers, Sister did a slow round of all her patients, taking their pulses, checking for herself their general conditions that she had just been given in the night senior's full, night report, before prayers. The opportunity allowed Sister and the patients to discuss in private their personal health, domestic and other problems. Mrs Ames never pressed for confidences and often with new patients, merely used her eyes, fingers and what the weather was doing outside.

To Mrs Ferrers, Sister said, 'As you were a bit muzzy when I passed on my trunk call to your mother-in-law last evening, I should tell you again how very sorry she is about all this, how much she appreciates your efforts to be with them today and how sorely you'll be missed. And Mrs Ferrers Senior said I was particularly to tell you she'll be writing to the children and your husband, and will be very tactful and you are not to worry about anything and get well soon.'

Mrs Ferrers thanked her politely, if perfunctorily, then noticed the wedding ring. 'I suppose your husband is one of the doctors, Sister?'

Sister smiled serenely. 'Yes. He's a Martha's man. I gather from your mother-in-law that Major Ferrers is now in India.'

'All this last year. Quite a break from Burma, but I expect he'll be back there soon.' She had to change the subject. 'Pity all these windows are blocked. From the sound of Big Ben this must be near the river. View must be worth seeing.'

'It is. Such a pity,' agreed Sister placidly. 'You don't know London well?'

'Not really. Of course I've been down a few times, but the last was – oh – when? Yes – first week of the war.'

'Quite a time.' Sister moved on to 34.

Miss Evers had been listening whilst eating her breakfast. She waited until Sister had reached 29 then leaned carefully to her right and used her 'in church' voice. 'I reckon Sister'd not be sorry to have her hubby in India.'

'I thought he's one of the doctors here?'

'Oh no, Mrs Ferrers. RAMC major with Monty's lot. Over there from D-Day. Never knew him, but lovely doctor, Daisy says and ever so nice looking and black hair like Dr Brown – he's the Irish one over the medical side that's always got a smile and a joke. Lovely black hair Dr Ames has, Daisy says, and married Sister when she was a staff nurse – make a lovely couple with Sister being fairish.' Miss Evers sighed romantically and pleasurably. 'Your hubby fairish, Mrs Ferrers? There! Knew it! I shouldn't wonder if poor Nurse Martin's young man's got nice dark hair – she's the very pretty one just come in with the penicillin Nurse Thane'll be giving with her, as Nurse Thane's having the wash – the little dark one with the staff nurse's belt and the eyes, up the middle sink far-side, see? Ever such good pals those two nurses are and nice for Nurse Martin seeing she's fretting cruel for her young man.' She explained why, then continued, 'Posts bound to have gone haywire seeing what must be going on over there, but soon have him home, we all tell Nurse Martin, and I do hope it keeps fine as this morning Sister's given her and Nurse Thane a ten-to-one off together special to go up west to buy something nice for her to wear to welcome him home. Engaged proper, they are and, like I always said to my customers, if you've got a friend you trust can't do better than have her help you choose — oh, I am sorry, Nurse Burton, dear! Would I like another slice of fried bread and tomato? Don't mind if I do!'

Mrs Ferrers was more interested than she expected in Miss Evers's revelations, as they had caused the first crack in her 'they don't know there's a war on' impression, gave her an immediate sense of fellow feeling with Sister, particularly, and this was her first experience of being a hospital patient. She had had her babies at home, and her previous encounters with hospitals had been limited to the ferrying and collecting of patients and their relatives in her own car from her local cottage hospital in her capacity as a driver for the Women's Voluntary Services. When not driving, she Dug for Victory, firewatched three nights a week, and single-handed ran her smallish house, large garden, and in the school holidays a cheerful home for her children whose overall welfare had been her sole responsibility for four years and nine months. Mrs Ferrers had accepted this as just one of those things, but never once had the acceptance lightened her continuous nagging anxiety for her husband and their children. Miss Evers's gossip was a bit of a break, she decided; something new to brood on, but she hoped the nice old bod wouldn't keep it up, as she, Mrs Ferrers, was actually feeling rather like the Wrath of God.

The normal ward routine progressed quietly and in an orderly fashion. The breakfast trolleys disappeared, the screen went up across the doorway for a bed-pan round, then came down at the first stroke of nine. The long white coats came and went, first on the medical side as physicians took precedence to surgeons, then the surgical; the elderly newspaperboy ambled all round; two or three chaplains of varying denominations; two or three young, fresh-faced girls in white, three-quarter length physiotherapists' coats, with muscular arms and hearty, hushed voices that uniformly reminded Mrs Ferrers of the games mistresses in her own and her daughters' boarding-school. Miss Evers quietly identified each in-comer to Mrs Ferrers, but to the latter's surprised relief asked no personal questions and did not tire her with more long spiels.

Miss Evers's innate sensitivity, even more than her experience as an old hospital hand and present doyenne of Alex patients, recognised the new neighbour she had categorised as a proper lady was bound to be fretting for her hubby and the kiddies in the snap on her bedtable and needed to take things quietly and have lots of nice little naps.

The mid-morning hot drinks' trolley had come and gone by eleven when Matron arrived on her daily round of every ward. Matron was a slight, still very pretty woman in her early fifties, and in her navy light woollen dress, white organdie collar and cuffs, and be-frilled lace cap that, as Sister's, had a lace bow under the chin, she struck Mrs Ferrers as oddly impressive. Sister escorted Matron and waited smiling placidly whilst Matron exchanged a few words with every patient.

'I'm glad to see you looking more than a little better this morning, Mrs Ferrers. Feeling a bit more comfortable? Good . . . Ah, Miss Evers! Still hard at it? My goodness that sweater has progressed since yesterday. . . .'

On most mornings, at some point, a long-white-coated pathologist strolled in carrying under one arm one of the smallish, oblong wooden boxes fitted with test-tubes and glass slides without which no pathologist on duty moved around the hospital. Invariably, upon entering a ward he (Martha's had no female doctors or medical students) nodded pleasantly to whoever was in charge, strolled on unescorted to the required bed, checked the name in the request form in his hand with that on the bedticket, then exchanged the time of day with its owner and murmured apologetically, 'May I have a drop of blood? Just a little prick – won't hurt – that's it – many thanks,' before strolling off waving his thanks to the desk – whether occupied or not.

Mrs Ferrers had again closed her eyes without being asleep, when she heard a strange, attractively deep murmur, 'I'll come back, Miss Evers. I don't want to wake her.'

'I'm not asleep, doctor.' Mrs Ferrers opened, then widened her eyes at the khaki shirt, tie and service trousers beneath the white coat. 'What's an MO doing in a civvy hospital?'

Charles smiled and put his wooden box on her bedtable. 'Just filling the odd gap. May I take a drop of blood from one finger? Just a little prick – won't hurt – that's it – thanks very much.'

She was too puzzled to let him go. 'I would have thought the chaps in Europe needed every MO they could lay hands on.'

'You could be right, Mrs Ferrers.' His smile didn't alter, but he glanced quickly around the ward. 'How are you feeling?'

'Bit beaten up below the belt, otherwise, fine, thanks. All I seem to do is sleep. It really is quite astonishingly quiet in here.'

'It is,' agreed Charles, exchanging brief glances with Miss Evers who enjoyed little chats with anyone with time to spare and had taken to beckoning him for one on his occasional visits to Alex. That these, though always prompted by professional requests, were of more than professional interest to him, was now an open secret on the grapevine, and to Miss Evers well before Daisy confided the grapevine's explanation. Miss Evers, as she told Daisy, had eyes in her head and no one had to tell her when a young gentleman was sweet on a young lady as all you had to do was watch the way he couldn't keep his eyes off her and very nice too! Miss Evers's generous heart enjoyed watching that nice Captain Bradley that she must remember to call Dr Bradley and that looked just like Gary Cooper in a white coat only perhaps not so good-looking but like they said, handsome was as handsome does. Always gave her a lovely smile when he came in these days, but not smiling now, she noted in their exchanged glances, and nor more was she. That one yesterday morning had done no harm, but – !

Mrs Ferrers had still not surfaced from her anaesthetic when just after morning prayers yesterday's only flying bomb within the hospital's hearing had switched off over the river and dived onto Martha's ruins. It had flattened the burnt-out Theatre Block 6, sliced off the top half of the mound of 7, strewn the length of the terrace with debris, blasted the replaced statue of King Henry VI once more from its plinth, and medicine and lotion bottles, test-tubes, bedpans, urinals, cups, mugs, jugs, teapots and so on from just about every open shelf in the standing blocks, but caused no lasting human damage. The noise had temporarily deafened all but the drugged in the neighbour-hood, but was a distant thunder-clap in Beaufort Street.

Charles was in the tube to Westminster when he heard from fellow passengers that poor old Martha's had copped it again. At Westminster Tube Station he charged stiffly, white-faced and tight-throated, up the steps, nearly knocking over the policeman who then told him Martha's luck had been in and Jerry's out. 'Got the wrong end, he did.' This hadn't stopped Charles racing as fast as his left leg allowed for the far-side pavement of Westminster bridge from where he had seen the flattened 6, and sliced off mound of 7. And after Dacey's, 'Not so much the one scratch or bit of grit in the eye for all he had what you might call a smashing time,' Charles had walked onto the terrace to see for himself and spent a long time looking down at the stone statue again on its back but now looking as if a razor had shaved off both slightly protruding blank eyes and two-thirds of the long, sharp, Plantagenet nose.

Miss Evers lowered the sleeveless sweater she was expertly cable-stitching as a 'thank you' for Mr Hall with wool she had unravelled from a long-sleeved navy jumper she had made herself pre-war and that Daisy had then washed and stretched to dry around the back of a hard chair in her room in the Nurses' Home. 'Would you have a moment, Dr Bradley?'

'I think so.' He moved to her bedside limping only slightly. 'What can I do for you, Miss Evers?'

'A big favour, doctor.' She held up the knitting whose required measurements she knew by heart. 'Could I try this against you for size? It's for my neighbour and he's a great tall gentleman same as you, doctor, but he's got more in the tummy – if you'll pardon the expression – and less in the shoulders. Six foot three, Mr Hall is. That you, doctor?'

Charles nodded, and over her head smiled at Sister smiling from the desk, and putting down his box held out his arms to the general amusement of all Alex.

'Thanks ever so, doctor and I'm really obliged and'll not ask what the weather's like up there, though as I tell Nurse Thane, temptation's wicked when you're on the small side like her and me.' She put down the knitting. 'Still nice and bright outside, is it, doctor?'

'Was, last time I looked,' said Charles, feeling the sun rise within him at the mention of Sarah's name.

'I am glad! Sister's given Nurse Thane the ten-to-one special to take Nurse Martin on a shopping spree – ' she added precisely why and the names of the West End department stores she had advised the nurses to patronise. 'Nice little break for them both.'

And for yours truly, my dear, thought Charles gratefully. Sarah had previously told him she had a two-to-five today and her absence at this hour had been convincing him she had disappeared to go on night-duty. If so she would vanish from his life for the twenty-one nights she would have to work before her first three nights off and after working eleven-hour nights most of her nights off she would want, and need, to spend in sleep.

'All set, Miss Evers?' He smiled widely. 'Fine. Be seeing you.' He waved to the ward as he left.

Mrs Ferrers had now noticed his slight limp. 'Has that doctor been wounded, Miss Evers?'

'Oh yes, dear. Can't see his left leg for the scars one of the theatre porters told Daisy, but doing ever so nicely — ' she sighed 'and you might well say more's the pity. Army'll have him back soon.'

'I expect so,' said Mrs Ferrers lapsing into silence and chiding herself on her unfailing ability to drop bricks by the ton.

It was about half an hour later, and Charles was back in the In-Patients' Lab, when that day's only flying bomb in the vicinity roared in up river, swung south over the hospital and about ten seconds later switched off its engine and dived at a wide, southern slant. In Martha's the explosion was only near-deafening and the objects upon shelves were only rattled. Charles's immediate reaction was, thank God she's up west, and then was immediately followed by, Christ! Our zone.

In Alex, Mrs Ferrers took longer than her fellow-patients to recover her breath and colour. 'That a buzz bomb, nurse?' she enquired of Nurse Yates who for some reason unknown to Mrs Ferrers was at her bedside.

Nurse Yates's mask hid her affronted expression. 'Yes. Actually, we call them doodlebugs. Comfortable?'

'Yes, thank you.'

'You don't look it. You've slipped down. We must get you higher.' She beckoned Nurse Burton and whilst the latter efficiently supported Mrs Ferrers's head and shoulders, Nurse Yates turned, shook up and re-arranged the pillows. 'We'll lift you up the bed. Just go limp, please and leave it to us. Up we go. How's that?'

'Very much more comfortable, thank you, nurse.'

The nurses exchanged a rare, communal glance. Of course she was much more comfortable. They weren't raw pros and anyway, even first-years learnt in their first three months in the wards how to lift bedpatients and make them much more comfortable. But as there was a limit to fraternisation, and that last one had dropped too close for the liking of either, they looked quickly away from each other and automatically towards the doorway, then promptly exchanged another kind of communal glance, before looking quickly at Sister at the desk. Miss Evers looked at the doorway and dropped three stiches.

Matron had returned with one of the youngest Office Sisters and in seconds had been joined by Sister Alex whose face was so suddenly drained of colour that her chubby cheeks sagged whitely. She and Matron disappeared to the dutyroom and the Office Sister sat down at the desk and began talking quietly to Nurse Grey, the senior nurse on duty. Miss Evers could not see that the dutyroom door was closed, but Nurses Yates and Burton, the two medical patients, and Daisy, arriving just then with the electric luncheon trolley from the main kitchen, had done so. Daisy instantly recognised the implications of that closed door and the Office Sister at the desk, and once she had pushed the heavy trolley into the kitchen, Daisy leapt, tight-lipped, for her best small teapot, the tea-caddy and boiling water urn.

All three nurses were now at the desk. Miss Evers glanced at them then mouthed to the patients opposite, 'Door closed?' and they nodded, unhappily. Though they had not been in long, they already knew that that door was only closed for consultations and bad news; and at this stage of a long war they knew that for Matron to have come in person bringing with her a relief Sister, could mean only one thing.

112

A strained silence fell over Alex and Miss Evers's dropped stitches lay un-picked-up on the turn-down of her top sheet. Mrs Ferrers sensed the sudden atmospheric tension and turning her head towards Miss Evers for enlightenment saw the tears in Miss Evers's eyes and asked no questions. She looked all around more closely and, having for so long been an active serviceman's wife and lived with fear for him, slowly she recognised why Matron had returned, and that the tension in the ward atmosphere was caused by communal grief. It was considerably later before she realised that she was now having her first glimpse into the patient-to-nurse and patient-to-patient bonds, but in that strained silence she found herself thinking, as so often elsewhere — the war levels us all. We're a jumble of women of all ages in here, she thought, and as far as I can tell I'm the only patient that thinks of the meal we're about to have as lunch and not dinner, but right now that couldn't matter less. My God, Kipling was so right! And God help that poor woman now — she'll go off-duty, of course, Mrs Ferrers decided as the telephone in the flat started ringing.

'Martha's miss?' The driver asked Sarah as Val, her golden hair floating to her shoulders, climbed into the back of his taxi. 'Which entrance?'

'Nurses' Home please.'

'Would you both be nurses, miss? Righty-oh!' He slammed off his clock. 'No fares for nurses, miss. In you go. Have you back in a jiffy.'

Sarah thanked him warmly and dropped onto the back seat by Val. 'Heaven bless London's taximen. I feel hideously guilty about stopping them as they never let us pay but if we hadn't just spotted this one you'd have had to carry me back.' She rubbed her ankles. 'My feet are killing me.'

'Sorry to take such ages choosing, but it's so difficult

always and as I was using your coupons too – '

'Panic over, Val.' Sarah flopped back, smiling. 'Stop flapping. That powder blue get-up is just you and will knock John for six.'

'You really think so? You don't think it's a bit tarty? I mean, I know he loves blue – '

'All Englishmen do – equate it with pretty,' said Sarah mentally chalking Charles another good mark for his individuality in admiring deep purple. 'John won't think that cross-over bodice tarty. Just – ' she wolf-whistled softly.

Val shook her head uncertainly at the string bag on her lap that contained unwrapped the blue rayon dress and matching jacket she had bought with her last birthday present money from her parents and the clothing coupons she and Sarah had hoarded for its purchase. [The annual adult civilian allowance was 32 and the outfit had required 17.]

Sarah watched her wearily. It was ten days from Sarah's last weekend off and the next wouldn't start until six tomorrow evening. The last thing she would have chosen to do this morning was to go shopping with Val, who had trouble making up her mind even over a pair of black lisle uniform stockings. Without me, thought Sarah, she'd now be returning empty-handed, as these days she's in too much of a flap over John to decide anything for herself. Heaven help us all when she has to choose her wedding – hold it!

It was then, in the back of the taxi turning into Trafalgar Square, that Sarah saw clearly the astonishing truth about Val and, having done so, all that astonished her was that it had taken her so many years to see it. Dumber than dumb, that's me, thought Sarah. Sticks out a mile. Val's genuinely anxious for John, but just plain terrified by the thought that when – if – he gets back, they'll marry. I know that for years she's been dreaming of this, but 'dreaming'. A lovely, lovely day-dream that poor old John's long incarceration has allowed to remain untarnished. He's her prince on a white charger who'll one day ride her off into the sunset – and perfect excuse for handing frozen mitts to Paddy and all the others who have panted after her at intervals throughout our training. Paddy and Coy are real – so's marriage – and that's what's really scaring her rigid. Poor Val. Oh, dear – what in hell can I do about it? I dunno . . . have to think . . . cope anon.

At the steps of the Nurses' Home the beaming driver accepted their thanks but not their offered tip and drove off waving his cap. 'God bless 'em all,' said Sarah, smiling and opening the front door.

'Been watching out for you, Nurse Thane! The portress rushed from her lodge. 'Office been ringing for you. Matron wants to see you soon as you're changed and before you go back on duty – and you best get back into uniform sharp, Nurse Martin. Most the day nurses off already gone back on though I've not heard of any coming in yet from the last one.'

'Last?' echoed Sarah, in shocked confusion. Twice in the past Matron had unexpectedly summoned her, first to break the news that David had been killed and then that her father had had a sudden, fatal coronary. Her mind registered rapidly – I've no one left apart from – and anyway – he isn't – 'Where did it drop, Miss Wells?'

'Back of Waterloo somewhere. Missed the station, I heard. No more.'

'Thanks.'

The two girls ran for the lift and began undressing once it had cleared the hall. They emerged into the top corridor in brassieres, pants and dangling suspenders and four minutes later the lift carried them down in neat, clean, uniforms.

As they raced into Central Hall they saw in the corridor ahead Paddy Brown looking as if he had just touched down

115

in flight and have to wave his arms to maintain balance, whilst urgently saying something to Charles Bradley, who was looking as if made of stone. The two men glanced their way, with very different expressions, then Paddy shot away, but not before his expression had rung all Sarah's mental alarm bells and evoked the thought — Paddy's passed the buck. 'What's the gen, Charles?' she demanded quietly.

He looked straight into her face. 'Bloody awful, I'm afraid. He got a double-decker at a bus stop. Twenty-three seriously injured on the way in. Eleven known dead. 'Minors', anyone's guess, but, sorry, that's not all.' He glanced at Val, then back to Sarah. 'Hugh Ames has bought it. Died of wounds sustained in action yesterday. Matron saw the telegram. She's told his wife and the Dean — so — we heard.'

Val buried her face in her hands. Sarah's upraised face was white and numb. She said mechanically, 'Matron's sent for me. I'm sorry. I must go. Thank you.'

He inclined his head and watched her walk quickly away, small, trim, straight-backed and crackling starch.

Val dropped her hands and muttered pathetically, 'Not Dr Ames too — oh, I just can't face it — I'm sorry, Dr Bradley, I just sort of can't — not on top of — I just can't!'

He looked very gently into her pretty, appalled face and wide, frightened eyes, and he thought, not unkindly, no, poor kid, you can't any more than Paddy just now — 'you tell 'em, Charlie, can't face 'em — not after old Hugh — one of us — '.

Charles said gently, 'I know, nurse. I do know.' And he felt as if he had spent his entire life saying those words in moments such as this.

That night, he again borrowed Paddy's room in the Doctors' House and, before he went over, he went out on the blacked-out terrace, but this time alone. He leant on the parapet at a point in front of Block 3 and even although

116

the darkness hid from him the newly ruined ruins and prone statue, he did not once turn his head in their direction. After the human faces he had had to look upon in the last several hours, it would have taken a loaded gun to force him to look now at that mutilated stone face.

He leant on the parapet for a long while, chain-smoking and staring down at the black river. When Big Ben struck twelve, he thought, thank Christ today's over, and knew it had been another that would haunt him for years. But he could not then know there would be other reasons for this and that whilst he was standing by London's river, the US 3rd Army under General Patton were crossing the Rhine in assault craft, or that, upon the day that had just died, the 23rd March, 1945, Martha's, London, had admitted its final air raid victims of the Second World War.

CHAPTER SEVEN

SOME of the screens were still up in Alex eight days later when Sister Alex returned from the one week's compassionate leave that she had refused to start until the evening of 23rd March. Some screens were red and some white. Some of the red screens were half-open at either side of bedheads; and on the bedtables across all the so-screened beds were smaller, white, improvised screens made by stretching bolster-cases longways, and fixing the ends in wooden book-holders clipped to the bedtables that, initially, had mostly been borrowed from other wards. Alex had four book-holders in stock; by the night of 23rd March, Alex had needed eighteen, for the five beds on the left and four on the right nearest the doorway.

When Mrs Ames returned to her ward, the medical line started at 7, with Mrs Jones, who had leukaemia and was back for another course of blood-checks and transfusions. The two pneumonias and Miss Evers had been transferred to semi-convalescent wards in the Hut in this Tuesday's normal convoy, and the surgical line of 'olds and newers' began with Mrs Ferrers, now in 31 and due to have alternate stitches and the much-shortened corrugated rubber drainage tube removed from her wound today. For the last two days all four terrace end beds had been empty; from the general post consequent on the admission of the last flying bomb casualties, 6 and 32 had been empty, and so, from yesterday, had been 2, 4 and 35, and from the small hours of this morning, 3 and 34.

Not eight days but a lifetime, reflected Mrs Ferrers glancing over the empty bed on her left at Miss Vickers's half-open screens. Mrs Ferrers now regarded Miss Vickers in 33 as an old chum, even though she only knew her by her voice. Only the staff and Mrs Harley, her sister and next-kin, had seen Miss Vickers's face.

Mrs Ferrers returned her gaze, but not her mind, to the clean pillowslip she was darning neatly and that Sarah had thankfully provided after Mrs Ferrers told her she wished she had some needlework with her. 'I loathe knitting, but love sewing.'

'Would you do some ward mending for us? Wonderful! It's always mounting and we never have time for it.'

They had become great friends; Sarah now knew of Major Ferrers's chronic prickly heat and detestation of army life and jungle warfare, 'In that order, my dear', and the names, ages, prowesses and idiosyncrasies of the four Ferrers children. Sarah had never mentioned Charles or her personal life to Mrs Ferrers, but, having been primed – and unconsciously taught – by Miss Evers, Mrs Ferrers, as she put it to herself, was keeping a weather eye on both parties and putting in the odd helpful word. Nice, quiet type with a good chin and steady eyes, Dr Bradley – that type made good husbands and fathers – she knew – married one. Nurse Thane was more than a poppet with eyes to turn any man's head, she was bright as a button and extraordinarily nice. If anyone rated a good chap it was her Nurse Thane, mused Mrs Ferrers, watching Sarah emerge masked and carrying a covered dressing tray from Miss Vickers's half-screens and cross over to those similarly shielding Mrs Donkin in 5. She didn't realise she had used that 'her' or that by the time that Sister Alex had finally been removed from duty by Matron on the evening before her week's compassionate leave, Mrs Ferrers had started thinking of the acting-staff nurse as Nurse Thane and not 'the little girl with wizard eyes'.

Upon that evening, after escorting Sister Alex, Matron had returned to go all round the ward with Sarah. Then, in the doorway, she said, 'Just one patient still to come from the theatre, Nurse Thane?'

'Yes, Matron. A Miss Amy Helen Vickers, age 48. Her sister with whom she lives is Mrs Harley and she has just left us after identifying the clothes Casualty sent us after sending Miss Vickers straight to the theatre. Mrs Harley is ringing Alexandra later tonight and coming in again tomorrow morning.'

'Thank you, nurse.' The telephone was ringing. 'I'll see myself out, Nurse Thane.'

'Thank you, Matron.' Sarah dealt with the telephone then put her head round the kitchen door. 'Theatre is ready for you to bring up Miss Vickers, Burton. Sorry, Daisy. Mind starting suppers for the "olds" alone?'

'Do you mind, nurse!' Daisy, songless and sombre, whisked from oven to electric trolley a huge dish of tripe and onions and a smaller one of creamed chicken.

Sarah shook her head at the rhetorical question and returned to the temporarily empty flat that was heavier with anaesthetic fumes than dust and echoed the chorused hissing and bubbling of eight sets of oxygen apparatus, and the sound of soft, helpless weeping filtering through the just-ajar bathroom door. In the bathroom with Nurse Yates were the parents that twenty minutes ago had identified as their daughter, Violet Smith, the young woman in 36, and as her friend, Margaret Edgar, the new patient in 1. Both worked in the Land Army in Wiltshire and had arrived yesterday to spend a week's holiday with Violet's parents.

Nurse Yates had given them brandy and tea and when Sarah silently looked in, one of Nurse Yates's hands patted Mrs Smith's shoulder and the other was on Mr Smith's wrist. Mrs Smith was on a hard chair, her husband in a wheel-chair, and the brandy had recovered a little colour in his dry-eyed, lined, agonised face. Only Nurse Yates saw the door open and she nodded briefly to say Mr Smith's pulse was recovering. Sarah thought clinically — as she dared think in no other fashion — it's mostly the men that pass out and the women that just weep — unless they are us, as all of us that have had to see what those evil machines can do to people's faces have long gone beyond weeping. She went quietly, swiftly back into the ward and stopping just beyond the screened near end, said quietly, but audibly to all the 'olds', 'I know you will all be relieved to know Matron has persuaded Sister to go off and that the gentleman who fainted is now recovering. Miss Elwes, the Office Sister you saw this morning, is taking over from Sister Alex for the next week and will be on at eight tomorrow morning. Suppers will be in soon, but I'm afraid may be a bit slow as Daisy's single-handed.'

Miss Evers spoke for all. 'Don't you worry about us, Nurse Thane dear. We're nicely.'

Nicely, reflected Mrs Ferrers, darning neatly and wincing mentally. Nine women, grossly mutilated, hideously disfigured, blinded, or semi-blinded. . . .

'Only the nine, Mrs Ferrers, dear — not like when he got the Market — forty-four in here that night and from what Daisy says more other nights than she's had Sunday dinners. Old Martha's had to get used to it same as the rest of us,' said Miss Evers in her 'in church' voice that held no trace of either bitterness or self-pity. 'Oh, look at the clock! Best get tidy. Mrs Hall's coming in at Visiting.'

'They'll have Visiting Time, tonight?'

'Oh yes, Mrs Ferrers. Routine.'

Routine.

'Oh yes, Mrs Ferrers dear, red screens always stay up round DILs — that's on the Danger List — and when — er — one's not so well, a third screen'll go up — routine. . . . '

Routine — white coats disappearing behind them reappearing from the screens round beds; Nurse Martin, Grey and Yates, apparently permanently behind those screens;

121

Nurse Thane going continuously from one set to another whilst simultaneously running the whole ward with only Nurse Burton's assistance; and Dr Bradley apparently running a blood-shuttle service as, whenever Mrs Ferrers saw him, he had either four full or four empty vacolitres of blood in his arms.

How can they take it? All so young – can't be one doctor over thirty and the nurses aren't much more than girls. What is this going to do to these girls? What has it already done?

Routine – so just before eight, 'Time for visitors to leave, please. Goodnight . . . goodnight . . . ' then all the ward's main lights off, red night lights on, the red-linen shaded-overhead desk light pulled down to a couple of feet over seated heads, the similarly covered bedhead lights behind the red screens left on, and in the darkened rose-coloured ward, Nurse Burton kneeling on her own and Nurse Thane at the desk, reading to the ward, 'Lighten our darkness we beseech Thee, Oh Lord, and by Thy great mercy defend us from all perils and dangers of this night. . . .'

Mrs Ferrers, lying in her shadowed bed, thought, I've never thought of it from this angle. I've always known about civvy air raid casualties – who hasn't? But I've never actually thought of it from this angle. I should have, but I didn't, and I don't know why – oh, but you do, Isobel, my girl! Let's face it – you hadn't the guts.

Guts. My God, Mrs Ferrers paused in her darning at Mrs Donkin's cheerfully raucous, 'Come to make me pretty with some nice yellow powder, Nurse Thane? You'll have a job, duck! Know what I am?' And to the tune of the old Cromwellian original, she sang lustily, 'I'm one of the ruins what 'Itler knocked about a bit – 'bout a bit – '

'Oy, Mrs Donkin!' interrupted Miss Vickers from across the ward, 'How about joining me and Nelson down Trafalgar Square? Done all right with his one eye, didn't he? I reckon if they shove us both up along of him we can have a nice game of three-handed whist and them pigeons better watch out.'

'Suits me, duck, but make it rummy. That's my game. Have the shirt off Nelson's back I will and I'll not stop there, duck, I can tell you – '

'Oy, oy, Mrs Donkin! Ladies present!'

'There I go again forgetting! Where's the soap and water to wash out me mouth, Nurse Thane, duck?'

A gust of laughter swept round Alex and out into the flat. Good as 'Gert and Daisy' on the wireless, those two; never a dull moment since they come off the DIL and hard to recall they were still SILs, agreed all their unscreened fellow-patients except Mrs Ferrers, secretly, as she was still too unaccustomed to Londoners to accept their natural habit of using laughter as a weapon in adversity.

'How do they do it, nurse?' she asked Sarah, when the latter was removing her alternate stitches and drain.

'God alone knows, Mrs Ferrers, but they always, somehow, find something to laugh at. Especially women.'

'Especially? Aren't men better patients?'

Sarah thought for a few moments whilst her sterile, brown rubber-gloved hands snipped with scissors and removed another stitch with artery forceps. 'I've found men very good patients, but women, generally, just that bit better, particularly in here.' She looked up and above the mask her eyes were bright with wonder and unshed tears. 'Nowhere, ever, have I had more wonderful patients than those I've nursed in Alex.'

'I think I get you, nurse.' Mrs Ferrers paused. 'What I don't get – and please don't get me wrong – is how can you take it? You told me the other day that, unlike Sister, you hadn't always wanted to nurse and only trained because of the war, so presumably you're not a born nurse – though no one would know it – so how do you manage to take all you have to do and see?'

123

Sarah looked at her. 'I don't know.'

'Do you get used to it?'

'No.' Sarah looked quickly downwards. 'Your wound is looking nice and healthy.'

'Glad you think so. I'd call it repulsive,' said Mrs Ferrers cheerfully, and then she changed the subject to her children.

Charles, taking another blood sample from Mrs Jones, over-heard, 'Freud would've had a field-day with my kids, Nurse Thane. When they were younger, the boys were always grabbing the girls' dolls and the girls their train-sets.'

He couldn't catch Sarah's murmured reply, but he was almost grateful Mrs Ferrers's temporary screens hid Sarah as this meant she genuinely hadn't seen him. In these last eight days he had noticed, at first in the hope that he was mistaken, and then with disturbing certainty, that Sarah was intentionally avoiding looking his way whenever he was in Alex, and literally going out of her way to avoid meeting him around the hospital. Instead of going off-duty as of old by Central Hall, she was now daily risking Sister Casualty's wrath by going out through Casualty. 'Nurse Thane, how many times must I tell you this is a Casualty Department through which visitors may enter and leave but NOT a public thoroughfare for nurses!'

Over the past weekend when she should have been free, owing to Sister Alex's absence and the new demands in Alex, Sarah had only had Sunday off and been promised an extra day off later. They had previously arranged to meet for lunch on Saturday and play the rest by ear. On Friday night Sarah had rung his flat to explain, and when he promptly suggested doing the same on Sunday, she had hesitated. Then, 'Charles I'm terribly sorry but I'm a bit whacked and would like to catch up on sleep. May I take another raincheck?'

'Of course,' he had said in the sudden hollow sensation

that this time she wouldn't and that he was beginning to understand why not.

The understanding had grown more comprehensive whenever he now walked through Alex. Whenever this was during the last eight days, he walked, ostensibly, looking straight ahead. But, being tall enough to see over red and white screens, he saw from the corners of his eyes the clean strips of gauze bandages holding the dressings in eyeless sockets, the black eyepatches over the single, missing eyes, the fine stitches cobwebbing the faces with enough skin left for this first repair, and the dreadful mutilation of others, that all were left open to the air under thick layers of penicillin powder because this method gave the best chances of healing, breathing and swallowing the saliva. The powder was applied four hourly, and the electric lighting made the yellow more garish and accentuated the horror, from which, since yesterday morning, five owners of the most mutilated faces had been released by death, mercifully so, in Charles' and others' opinions.

Walking through Alex had become for Charles walking through yet another corner of hell. The knowledge that the girl he loved with every fibre of his being had to spend eleven hours daily in that hell had so turned the knife that in these last eight days for the first time in years he had found himself mentally praying: Please, if You exist, let this lay-off stick for her sake. . . . He took no personal credit for the unbelievable fact that for the last full week London's skies had been quiet by day and black by night. No dust clouds, no smoke clouds, no pink splashes on night clouds, anywhere over Greater London or anywhere else in the UK. He took no personal credit, but he was devoutly thankful for all this, even although it had come too late to prevent that last flying bomb's carnage wrecking his personal hopes.

It figures too bloody plainly, he thought, walking slowly and with no limp, back to the In-Patients' Lab.-

125

Freud, of course, would write off her changed attitude as straight fear of sex. Far too specious, that one! What's happened to her is that her emotions have taken such a battering that finally they've been battered punch-drunk. Whether she knows that or not I don't know, but I do know that right now she recognises that she is incapable of taking on-board any more when she's off-duty. On the job she'll go on taking on what she has to because she's got to — and she's the girl she is. I wish to Christ I could help her but I don't know how, now that my hanging around is the last thing she needs — as you were! Could be the time has come to have a quiet word with Prof Pathology. . . .

Later that same day, he had that word. A few nights later, in the first week in April, he rang Sarah in the Nurses' Home. His call was put through to the telephone in the top-floor corridor that was on a wall shelf about ten yards from the door of Sarah's room. He wasted neither time nor words. 'I hope I haven't got you out of bed but I've some gen I want to give you. My Board was shifted forward. I'm cleared. Pushing off in the morning.'

She had been in bed but not asleep. She said abruptly. 'This is straight telepathy. I was just thinking about you.' Then she realised what he had said. 'The Medical Board's passed you fit for active service? When?'

'This morning.'

'Why so soon? You should have two more weeks.'

'No. Ten days. You know the Army. When did it ever stick to doing what it said it would?'

She knew this needed more thought, but lacking the necessary energy, had to let it go. Temporarily. 'Where are they posting you?'

'South-east England, tomorrow, but as I gather mopping up Europe's being hellish messy, my guess is over the water in a day or so.'

'What'll be your general address? And what's your Army number?'

He hadn't thought she would want this, but kept his unexpected surge to hope under firm control. 'Got something to write on?'

'Hold on while I get it.' She dived for her room and was back in seconds and breathing more rapidly than the exercise justified. 'Your Army number first, then the next bit.'

He had had time for thought. 'Listen, Sarah, you – er – you must know I'd very much like to hear from you, but as I know the set-up here – do you honestly want the fag of writing?'

She frowned at the blank wall behind the telephone and at herself. I've been a heel to him lately, she thought, and, though that wasn't intentional, it was unfair and unkind. 'Yes, I do.' She was firm. 'Gen, please.'

He gave his Army number. 'I'll send you the next bit when I'm sure of it. I don't want a letter from you chasing me round Europe and ending up lost. If the Army can lose anything, sure as hell it does. I could even be back before any letter has time to reach me. None of the chaps I've spoken to today seemed to have the foggiest what's actually going on where – apart from the Yanks and Russians having met up somewhere.'

'Paderborn. Paddy read about it in *The Times* a couple of days ago and told Val Martin he thought it damned funny they should've met up on April Fool's Day, and she told me. Hey – that reminds me – do me a favour?'

'If I can, of course. What?'

'Thanks. This. If you do get over the water, could you keep your eyes and ears open for any gen on Val's fiancé – got something to write with?'

'At the ready.'

'Good.' She gave John's full name, rank, old unit, and the number of his prison camp. 'I don't know his Army number. I'll get it tactfully out of Val and let you have it. She hasn't heard from him since Christmas, so if you do run

127

into any liberated Allied POWs could you ask around and, if you hear anything, let me know?'

Charles thought of, but didn't voice, one item concerning Allied POWs of the Germans that he had heard about this morning. 'I will.'

'Thanks a lot. Anything I can do for you this side? Like about your flat?'

'I don't think so, thanks. I'll just lock and leave the flat. I paid-up in advance. Mine till the lease runs out.' He didn't say when this would be. 'I hope I'll be back there shortly.'

Knowing exactly what that last remark meant, she thought fast and spoke slowly, 'I'd like to see it, then.'

Hope exploded through his control. 'I'd like that very much as – er – you know.'

'Yes.'

'As – er – you also know I love you like hell?'

'Wondered.'

'Don't. Fact. May as well hand on another – I want to marry you, one day, Sarah, but as that has to stay on ice – mind my telling you?'

'No.'

Never in his life had that monosyllable given him such pleasure. 'Good.' he said quietly, 'bloody good. Well – er – that wraps it up, pro tem. Take care of yourself. See you around, sometime and – '

'Take care of yourself, Charles – ' she put in quickly to stop him ringing off before she had the chance, 'and don't forget the way back and thanks for everything and all the best. I'm glad we met.'

'Snap. I'll be in touch,' he said and rang off feeling as if one of his limbs had been torn off.

Sarah sighed wearily and very sadly and, as she replaced the receiver, thought, thank God he couldn't salute me and forgot to say 'Cheers'.

APRIL, 1945

CHAPTER EIGHT

'SARAH, wake up!' Val threw aside the two pillows lying over the back of Sarah's head and shook her shoulders. 'Wakey-wakey!'

Sarah, sprawled face downwards, groaned, 'Get lost, Val. It's my extra day off and – '

'I know it is, but you must wake up!' Val shook harder. 'President Roosevelt's dead and you've got a huge letter that Dacey says was handed in by a Mr Mackenzie forty minutes ago and that this Mackenzie was in the same year as your brother and I'm sure the letter is actually from Charles Bradley as the handwriting on the envelope is exactly like his on returned path. forms.'

Sarah twisted around like a blue-and-white striped eel, pushed the hair from her sleep-flushed face and forced open her sleep-gummed eyes. She had just slept for fifteen hours. 'Huh?'

It was a quarter-past-ten in the morning and Val, just off for a ten-to-one, had taken down Sarah's blackout screen, dropped her cloak in Sarah's armchair, and stood over her waving a long, thick, buff envelope in her mingled agitation at being the bearer of bad and – what wishful thinking convinced her was – good news. Val had recently been plunged in gloom over the cooling of Sarah's relationship with Charles. She had previously been delighted to the extent of confiding to her mother on one of her weekly days off that she invariably spent in her parental home in Dorking, that she was sure there was something in it. Mrs

Martin had also been delighted. She thought Sarah Thane a nice gel, and to her Edwardian mind the only acceptable future for any nice gel was in marriage to a nice young man with good prospects and what could be nicer than a nice young doctor – as she had previously repeatedly observed to her husband in private since early in 1942. . . . Of course, without doubt, dear John couldn't be nicer and had proved himself the right stuff by leaving his father's farm in Kenya and coming home to join-up in his father's old regiment, but it couldn't be denied that they really knew so little about him and his people and with so many nice young doctors around St Martha's – but there it was. . . .

Val repeated herself but less incoherently. 'President Roosevelt died of a cerebral yesterday. It's in this morning's papers and – '

'God, how bloody!' Sarah flopped back and closed he eyes. 'Done so much and won't see the end.'

'Sarah, sit up or you'll go back to sleep!' Val dropped the letter to haul Sarah into a sitting position much more vigorously than had she been a patient, but using the same basic technique. She jammed the pillows behind Sarah's shoulders and against the polished teak bedhead. 'You've got a letter to read. From Charles Bradley, I'm sure. Isn't this his writing?'

Sarah blinked at the offered envelope and was suddenly wide awake. 'Yes. But no censor's stamp or – '

'I've been telling you – it was delivered by hand by this Mr Mackenzie who was in Charles and David's year. He kept the taxi taking him to King's Cross waiting whilst he handed it in to Dacey. Dacey knew that you were off and I'd be off at ten and hung around to catch me leaving Alex as I'd get it to you quicker than if he passed it on to Matron's office. Dacey said this Mackenzie's a captain like Charles and when they were first posted overseas they sailed on the same troopship, but poor Mr, or rather Captain Mackenzie was a POW sort of long as John, only Captain

Mackenzie was flown back with another batch of ex-POWs last evening after spending a couple of days or whatever in some dispersal camp in Germany – and I'm sure there he ran into Charles and Charles asked him to deliver this. All he actually said about it to Dacey was could he make sure you got it. Do open it, Sarah!' There was a new, hesitant eagerness in Val's face. 'There might be something about John in it. I mean – the other days when you sort of asked casually for John's number and old unit and all that, wasn't it to pass on to Charles sometime in case he sort of met someone who might have some gen on John?'

Sarah knew Val too well to be surprised by her occasional moments of accurate personal insight, but on this occasion Sarah was disconcerted. 'Sort of,' she agreed vaguely, and was uncomfortably conscious of her very recent and growing unease over John and that had no connection with the insight of Val she had discovered in a taxi turning into Trafalgar Square. Today was the 13th April; for the last few days the first batches of released British POWs had been flown back from Germany and the few amongst them with sisters, fiancées and girlfriends in the Home had been ringing up unexpectedly, joyfully, from RAF stations in the Midlands and East Anglia. Sarah had been containing her unease with the truthful reminder that there were thousands still to come, but after the only letter she had yet had from Charles, the thickness of the envelope in her hand disturbed her greatly. His first letter, posted in London on the morning after his farewell telephone call, had reached her in that evening's post, covered two-thirds of one side of one page and yet said so much, so gently, that she had replied to it, as briefly, in her two-to-five upon the following day. She had told no one that she had heard from Charles and certainly not that her three paragraphs had taken her two hours. She suspected, rightly, Charles's had taken him about the same. This one not only felt, but was, different.

133

'I need a fag, first, Val. On my dressing-table with matches and ashtray — sling over my scissors whilst you're about it. Help yourself to a fag and sit down.'

Val obeyed with relieved docility, but before lighting her cigarette, she removed and carefully folded her clean apron. She left on her cap. It was a strict rule that nurses in uniform dresses must wear caps in the Home even when off-duty and in the privacy of their own, or friends' bedrooms. Owing to Home Sister's insistence upon maintaining this rule, it was her highly unpopular custom to enter nurses' rooms unexpectedly, without knocking, and if no offender was present, to say, 'So sorry, nurse, thought your room was empty. Just checking the cleaners have finished,' and back out. That smoking in uniform was equally forbidden was more easily ignored by the quick-handed in the company of an off-duty friend in civvies or night-wear to provide an explanation for the nicotine smoke. Val sat on the edge of Sarah's bed and kicked off her shoes. One rule no Home Sister or Matron of Martha's had ever attempted to enforce was that off-duty nurses, in or out of uniform, must wear shoes in the Nurses' Home.

Sarah held the lighted cigarette in her lips whilst she slit the envelope and took out three quarto-sized RAMC case history sheets closely written on both sides. The first page, dated and timed '11/4/45 23.30', began 'My dear Sarah . . .'

She read intently, in silence, and often returning to re-read more than once a phrase, sentence, or paragraph. The long sleep had returned the roundness of youth to her small face, and in the faded pyjamas that had been her brother's, she could have been a schoolgirl. Pyjamas cost money and clothing coupons. Being a fourth-year, Sarah earned forty pounds a year, and since her father's pension had died with him, this was all she had to live on. She had within her the same seam of granite realism that existed in Charles and that both had first recognised in each other on the steps of the fallen statue in the blackness of M-night. That quality in both had frequently, severally, been dismissed as callousness by those who preferred the comfort of facile explanations. Charles, once separated from Sarah's physically disturbing presence and the inevitable confusion this caused his emotions, had recognised their mutual realism afresh, when writing to her upon the night before last. And Sarah, reading what he had then written, with her mind cleared by sleep, was having not only her own refresher in this context, but also seeing Charles himself in a bright light. But she was not yet aware of any of this, as her conscious concentration was polarised by the main subject matter of his letter.

Val watched her eagerly, anxiously. Then the eagerness and anxiety faded from her pretty face that was pale with fatigue on this fourth day from her last day off. She stubbed out her cigarette, moved unnoticed to the armchair, flicked her cloak to the floor and, sitting sideways to protect her cap bow, swung her legs over one arm, relaxed against the other, and in less than a couple of minutes her head tilted forward and she was deeply, silently, asleep. And Sarah, a couple of yards off in the low, comfortable, divan-type bed lined against one wall and backed into the corner farthest from the window, was mentally, literally, over a thousand miles away amongst British soldiers of all ranks and in old uniforms that had survived years in prisoner-of-war camps and were wet, cold, filthy and lice-ridden and hung upon the undernourished bodies of their owners being marched from east to west across Europe.

'Marched for one thousand miles in mid-winter after year of malnutrition if not semi-starvation,' wrote Charles.

Jerry was determined to get them away from the Russians to use as hostages with our lot or the Yanks. In the early stages, after every few days on the march, they had a rest-day, but as the Russians moved in faster from the east, their rest-days grew sparser and on he marched them – the well, the walking-wounded, the wounded, the sick (pneumonias/TBs/gangrenes/dysenteries/jaundices/et al.). Inevitably, some had it, but not as many as could have been had not all known they were moving west and over the last hill – home run. Hamish Mackenzie, a Martha's man, who gave me most of all this – incidentally, he's the dark, thin chap two down on my right in your photo of the '38 line-up – told me, 'I was lucky. The kick-off from our camp was 20th January, but I only walked till middish March and then had three weeks with the sick in a train. Not a proper sick-train. No equipment. Just old cattle-trucks and vans stacked with sick. Handy break for me as my boots, like most, had fallen apart. One of the two RAMC NCOs walking with me from scratch – hellish good chaps – managed to scrounge me a pair of Yank boots – brown – splendid pair but too small so I passed them on to his mate. . . .'

The top sash of Sarah's anti-blast papered window was open and a breeze from the river lazily lifted the pale blue cotton curtains she now opened last thing at night. The blackout screen had to be left up. London's blackout regulations remained unchanged, as did Sarah's habit of sleeping face down with the pillows over the back of her head and her father and brother's photographs, a powder compact and comb wrapped in her uniform cloak in a quickly available bundle under her head. These nocturnal arrangements had been hers since the day staff had been allowed to sleep in their rooms instead of in the bunks in basement dormitory shelters as insisted upon during the first months of the V1s, and during the earlier blitzes. For reasons neither specified, nor needed, authority had lifted the last order fairly shortly after the rockets began arriving, and from then left the choice of sleeping accommodation to the individual. A few day staff still used the basement bunks, but all Sarah's set had returned to the top-floor rooms that were their prerogative as the senior set and had the double advantages of being furthest from Home Sister's ground-floor bedroom and office, and having windows overlooking the broad, concrete, parapet-edged area that ran all round the building. In peace, it had been the nurses' roof-garden, and in war, at varying times, strictly out-of-bounds for months.

This had now been back-in-bounds for over two weeks, but until the present week had remained empty of lounging nurses as it had for years been empty of potted plants, shrubs and deck-chairs. In that Home, as elsewhere in London, it had taken time to accept that yesterday's quiet, last night's undisturbed sleep, could, just possibly, mean it was all over. Only just possible. According to the newspapers and wireless news, Jerry's back was to the wall and the wall was cracking, but it wasn't down yet, and whatever Jerry was, he was, above all, a fighting man, so if he'd got a V3 up his sleeve, this was when he'd use it on London . . . Well, I mean, nurse, know what the V stands for — Vergeltungswaffe — that's what and what that means in good English is Revenge Weapon . . . best take it softly, softly . . . best wait and see. . . .

Slowly, once again, in the public parks the paths and stretches of grass most distant from public shelters and Tube stations were beginning to fill with strollers and baskers in the April sunshine and there were strollers along the embankments and on the bridges' and other pavements. And those on the pavements of the road running past the hospital were again glimpsing nurses in and out of uniform, leaning on the parapet above and looking out at the great vistas of London opened to them by the missing hospital blocks in front, and the acres of missing buildings at the back of their Home.

This was another sunny day. The gulls floated on the breeze, the huge balloons swung placidly on their distant anchors and their long cables glinted in the sunshine as if celebrating their present superfluity. In Alex, the terrace doors were fixed open and the four beds at the terrace end and first five on either side of the doorway were empty. Mrs Ferrers was now convalescing with her in-laws near Godalming; Miss Vickers and Mrs Donkin were in neighbouring beds in a Hut ward and would shortly be transferred together to the most renowned civilian Plastic Surgery unit in southern England. Margaret Edgar and Violet Smith had died upon the morning and evening of the same day last week.

Earlier that evening, Sarah blanket-bathed Violet and changed her dressings. Violet's voice was so weak that Sarah bent her face to a couple of inches from what had been lips. 'Ta, Nurse Thane – feels lovely.' Violet's frail hand groped blindly for Sarah's arm and gripped weakly. 'You been ever so kind, nurse – all of you – ever so kind – ' she mumbled, then added more.

'Violet, dear, I'm terribly sorry, but I couldn't catch that last thing. Can you say it again?'

The frail hand let go to pat Sarah's arm gently. 'Just – ta – ever so – ' was Violet's barely audible and last utterance. A few minutes later she slid into sleep, and within an hour it had altered to coma, and then death.

Much later that evening, Sister Alex said privately to Sarah, 'I've never nursed a more gallant patient, but I couldn't have wished her one more hour, five more minutes, of life.' There was no placidity in her eyes or voice. 'When I took the day report to Matron just now she said Violet could prove to have been Martha's last fatal casualty of this war – please God may Matron be right. If she's not, Thane, I honestly don't know how I could face nursing through another onslaught, but I expect I'll manage somehow – like the rest of us.'

Sarah, speechless with distress, nodded briefly and knew that Sister understood her silence.

Charles, too. Charles too, and not only me, thought Sarah, lowering his letter, looking for a long time at Val's sleeping face and then for as long at Charles's penultimate paragraph:

You'll now have spotted just why I've spelt so much out and if you think a glimpse at the general picture will help Val and want to show her all or any of this, please go ahead. I think – hope – it may help her and that you'll understand why I do, and how much I dislike, offering you the buck. OFFERING ONLY. If you would rather leave it with me, just let me know and I'll write to her, stat. . . .

Sarah glanced up, tense with distress, and knowing, as Charles had known, that when such news had to be given the kindest way was from a great friend in privacy. But Val slept on. Sarah shook her head at her thoughts, then turned back to re-read the whole letter and, as before, to keep returning to certain parts.

David liked H.M. and so did – do – I. He was always a very decent chap, quiet type and neat as hell. From all accounts but his own, he's done a tremendous job for the chaps in his camps in Italy, Poland and East Germany plus on the march when, for obvious reasons, Jerry let him keep a medical diary and in it he managed to slip in a personal one mainly in med. Latin or braid Scots. He's translated these for me. One, after 10 days on the march, translated, 'Damn good night. Warm. Kipped down in pig-sty.' I asked, where pigs? 'Slept with us, man. Splendidly bloody warm, those pigs. Even unfroze the mud. . . .'

Lower down that page:

H.M. said on the march they got rations most days – not every day – but most, then he grinned. 'One day we

139

had meat. Not sure what meat, still meat in a turnip stew – damned good meal that day – even had our DILs deciding to last out the night. Our usual rations didn't do much for them but even so our sick did a hell of a lot better than the Russian and Yank sick. I had a few spells with both. Jerry gave the Russian sick no rations whilst I was with them and he doled my Yank sick one loaf for every 17 chaps per day. I tried raising hell and got nowhere – of course we shared our rations with both lots which didn't go far but was better than nothing . . . '

Over that page:

Sarah, I'm sorry to remind you of the date coming up, but I'm doing so as, obviously, the more one can see of a picture the more clearly one gets the general perspective. So, straight from H.M.'s diary: '23/3/45. Kick-off, 0200 hrs. Marched 40 kilometres to Berg Kerchen, near Ratibon – big fort there – again night in barns, 200 men each barn, no washing facilities, sanitation outside under armed guard. Numbers of sick increasing.

'24/3/45. Only a few kilos today. Roads bad. MOs billeted with sick all on bare boards in cold attics.

'25/3/45. This morning had to leave 7 of our advanced TBs in local Lazarett (German military hospital). Hellish leaving them but none could go on and, fortunately, this time Lazarett accepted them. Night in cow-shed, but no cows, so very cold.

'26/3/45. Sick numbers increasing. Pneumonias, TBs, jaundices, sore feet, endless dermatitis from lice/scabies, plus plain bloody exhaustions. Damned unpleasant day. Took me five hours to persuade local Lazarett to take 8 of our 40 DILs, had to take over 32 on. Kipped down in barrels tonight. Very cold but rumours flying round that tomorrow our sick'll be shifted to a train. . . . '

On the next page:

H.M. said on the march he saw little of the indigenous population and that most of those he did see looked the other way. 'But one morning on the sick-train after we'd been parked in a siding 36 hours, a youngish, blonde type – very snappy piece – gave us a huge can of hot soup before our guards warned her off. She was damned kind and brave as she took a hellish risk of being shot.'

Later, he said, 'We knew the show was closing when Jerry suddenly dished us Red Cross rations and 16 fags per man. Same again next day plus 1 extra fag. By then they had got all our sick out of the train and into a barn, marched on all the rest, and detailed a few RAMC to stay with our sick that included my Sgt T., Cpl J. and self. My bed was the MI [medical inspection] table – wooden planks on trestles and quite comfortable if my lice hadn't kept me awake.'

Again, Sarah, from his diary:

'7/4/45. Odd day. Not much sleep for any of our sick last night as rumours insisted Allies getting nearer and those heavy guns we heard during afternoon, until stopped by Jerry fighter-bombers, were our guns. Then a few hours quiet till 0100 today. Heavy gunfire opening up behind us and shells coming over. At 0430 our guards got us up to get our sick into slit-trenches, did so and stayed put hours. All morning fighter-bombers low overhead, then suddenly gone and we heard machine and light gunfire coming from the valley just beyond our trenches. 1500hrs. All quiet. Decided to investigate with Sgt T. and Cpl J. as self-ordered escort party. Climbed out of trench and discovered we were surrounded by U.S. troops on foot backed by tank-carriers and half-tanks. For a wee while we all looked at each other, then they said something to us in American

141

and we said something to them in English. I then told them we had had no new casualties amongst our chaps from today's show and after they had lifted out our sick and dished their K-rations to all of us, Sgt T. said to me, "Right sir. That's it."'

Sarah lowered the letter and for two or three minutes tared at the gulls floating past her window and then at the till sleeping Val, before reading on:

H.M. was swept into the bag just before the second fall of Tobruk in June '42. This was when Rommel's tanks went straight through a British battalion. The vehicle he and Sgt T. were in was suddenly cut off and surrounded by Jerry tanks and being un-armed non-coms, they'd had it. They were taken by lorry to Benghazi and to a prison camp that H.M., an expert in this context, had what he rates the filthiest sanitation to beat all. After a few days, he was flown to Italy and Sgt T., being an OR [Other Rank], was later shifted by sea. On H.M.'s aircraft, a three-engine Italian job, were several other British officers and one was Val Martin's fiancé. [He gave John's full name, Army number, rank and unit.] They went to the same Italian camp and after Italy packed it in were shunted north by rail in the same cattle-truck and landed in the same camps first in Poland, then E. Germany. It was in the last that H.M. met up again with Sgt T. who, with his mate Cpl J., had been shifted from an OR camp to help with the sick officers. Main sick, diphtheria and dysentery. 'Always endemic, those two,' said H.M., 'and John had dip. and, though he managed to throw it off, it didn't do him much good. The poor chap was never quite the same again and consequently a sitting duck for TB.'

Yes, Sarah, I'm afraid you know that's coming. John was one of the 7 advanced TBs that H.M. had to leave in a Lazarett on 25th March and, in his medical opinion, John was a DIL with both lungs gone and, at the outside, another 48 hours and probably less. There has not yet been an official confirmation of his death from Jerry, but even without what's presently going on over here, it's still too early for that. With Jerry's records being literally − inter alia − blown to hell, could be weeks, and more likely months before the official confirmation gets through.

I thought hard before writing this. Some might say I'm jumping the gun. I wish to Christ I didn't know that I am not. John won't be coming back, poor chap, and it seems to me too tough on Val to leave her waiting upon a hope that doesn't exist for − very likely − months. She's a sweet kid, but even if she weren't I'd write this as I wouldn't wish that kind of agony on anyone. I've talked this over with H.M. and he agrees and says I can tell Val from him that John was a damned good chap, strong in all but health, and that her letters were the shots in the arm that kept him going until his health, but not his guts, ran out.

If you do tell Val, please tell her I am so sorry.

That's all for tonight. Some other time I'll tell you about my present joint that's a combination of Oxford Circus in the rush-hour, a C.C.S. [Casualty Clearing Station] and dirty great de-lousing unit.

I miss you very much.

Take care of yourself, please.

Yours,

Charles.

P.S. I'm going to ask H.M. to hand this in to Cas. on his way home to Scotland. He's being flown back to the UK tomorrow and has to go through London, so it'll save time and the censor's blue pencil. God knows how many KRRs [King's Rules and Regulations] we'll break, but he won't give a damn and nor do I. Goodnight. C.

MAY, 1945

CHAPTER NINE

'THAT's all I've to tell you about today, nurses. I hope you have a good night.' Sarah looked up from the open ward log book from which she had been reading and slid the book to the night senior sitting on her right to mark the official moment of transfer from day to night staff. She had been verbally enlarging on the day report: 'Incidentally, Nurse Mayhew, if Ike makes up his mind before the night's out, put it in your tomorrow morning's written report.'

Nurse Mayhew, a fourth-year one set junior to Sarah's, looked vaguely amused and, as her junior sitting facing them across the desk, very tired. They were into their third month on nights in Alex and, respectively, eleven and eight from their last three off. 'Thanks for the reminder, Nurse Thane. I'd forgotten peace could break out before morning.' She scribbled a note to herself on one of the strips of scrap paper dogclipped together to serve as a memo pad, in case she forgot again.

The night junior thought aloud in a murmur, 'I suppose it'll make a difference.' She heard herself and blushed. She was in Nurse Burton's set, but lacked the latter's self-confidence. Sarah and Nurse Mayhew exchanged glances and without further comment flicked down their neatly up-folded apron skirts and rose from their chairs. During the three months in last winter when Sarah had been Alex's night senior, Nurse Mayhew had been on days in Casualty.

Alex was ready for the night; the main lights were off, red night lights on; eleven linen-shaded bedhead lights glowed over today's post-operative patients and the shaded pulled-down light cast a crimson pool over the desk. As always, the ward darkness was rose-coloured and in the shadows of the walls and bricked-in windows the unlit beds were tinged with pink. The terrace doors had been open all day, but in war and peace were locked at night. Throughout Sarah's training, the hospital had never had any nocturnal human intruders, but on any warmish late spring peacetime night, an open groundfloor door was an open invitation to moths, other insects, stray cats, and — according to cherished, apocryphal legend used to freeze further the blood of night juniors still reeling from their first encounters with the nocturnal cockroaches in ward kitchens — rats from the river.

Sarah said, 'I'll see myself out, Nurse Mayhew,' and called quietly, 'Goodnight, ladies. Sleep well.'

A chorus answered, ''Night Nurse Thane. See you when the war's over!'

In the small hours of the morning the combined Chiefs of Staff had received a telegram that read, 'The mission of this Allied Force was fulfilled at 3 a.m. local time May 7th 1945 Eisenhower.' But the official public announcement that all hostilities had ceased in Europe and that General Eisenhower had accepted Germany's unconditional surrender had not yet been made. All day, all over London, on pavements and station platforms, in shops, offices, trams, buses, tube and railway carriages, strangers had asked strangers 'Come yet?' All day in Casualty over the lodge telephones Dacey had been forced to reiterate, 'Not knowing, can't say,' before adding in the tone of one privy to military secrets, 'Mind you, I did hear old Hitler made a shocking mess down his bunker when he blew his brains out May Day, but not much else he could do seeing Berlin got took next day and if you ask me, poor old Jerry's getting as browned-off standing around holding out his hand for his cards to be stamped as we are waiting for old

Ike to get on with the job.'

Nurse Mayhew had begun her first night round and was moving from bed to bed, and the junior had disappeared into the kitchen to put on the milk and hot water urn for her first night drinks round, before Sarah had collected her cloak from the aseptically tidy flat bathroom. And already, Alex's habitual nocturnal atmosphere was permeating the flat with the mingled aromas of carbolic soap, talcum powder, hot rubber undersheets, ether, iodoform, heating milk, stale cigarette smoke, and, tonight especially, a strong lacing of anaesthetics.

Sarah stopped in the outer doorway to look up the flat and into the ward where only the four terrace end beds were empty. The ending of London's air-war had never been officially announced, but for the last three weeks the 'ten empty beds nightly' order had been ignored, the convoys to the country small, and Martha's, London, had recommended admitting acute as well as emergency cases. The night staff were in for a heavy night, thought Sarah, but just routine heavy. No dust clouds in Alex tonight; no grey faces and grey blankets; no hideously mutilated faces; no little white screens on bedtables; no 'UNKNOWN's on white labels; no 'Do you recognise this as hers?'; no Daisy singing softly in the kitchen, 'You Are My Sunshine'. But all this morning and all this evening until she went off at eight, Daisy had sung softly in the kitchen, 'I Don't Want To Set The World On Fy-er'.

I should thank God, thought Sarah, turning away, and if I could believe it, I would. Cope with that, anon. . . .

The 'ten empty beds' order had first been dropped during the two extra days off together that Matron had given Val after Sister Alex had told Matron the news that Sarah, in private, had given Mrs Ames.

'Thane, I'm so sorry. Poor girl. Poor boy. I'll speak to Matron. I'm sure she'll give Martin some time off, even

149

though only wives or blood-relatives officially rate compassionate leave. Leave it to me.'

It had been at Val's request that Sarah had told Sister, their set, and then, at Sarah's suggestion, Dacey, 'Yes, Sarah, yes – Dacey'll tell – people – and then no one will ask me – things. I couldn't face that – I just couldn't – oh, dear – poor John – oh, dear – oh, Sarah – I can't face it.'

'Not yet, Val, dear. Not yet. One day.'

Dacey had said, 'You leave it to me, Nurse Thane – and you will tell Nurse Martin – well, I mean, you'll know what I mean. . . .'

On the day after Dacey said that Val had gone home and Paddy Brown stopped Sarah in the ground corridor.

'Just checking some gen,' drawled Paddy. 'Someone told me Val Martin's intended has bought it with TB. Pukka?'

'Not officially verified, but I'm afraid I'm sure of it.'

He nodded to himself. 'My boss was just saying Hamish Mackenzie knew his medicine.'

'He knows more now.'

'That's a fact.' He hesitated, then nodded brusquely, 'You'll not believe the one damned word, Sarah, but I'm damned sorry about this turn-up.'

She looked straight up into his narrow, tense face. 'Don't sell yourself short, Paddy. Of course I believe you. We're both fond of Val and though neither of us knew her John, what the hell difference does that make?'

He smiled with his lips. 'Remind me to borrow a tin hat next time you pat me on the head.' He thrust back his long black forelock and the forced smile and a little tension vanished. 'How's she taken it?'

She met his troubled eyes. 'As you'd expect.'

'I believe you. The poor lovely girl.' He looked briefly at the floor. 'I'm glad Hamish Mackenzie has made it back in the one piece and if but a tenth of Dacey's gen is pukka, I'm damned glad it wasn't me wearing the boots that fell apart.'

150

'All pukka and I only gave Dacey the bare bones.'

'My boss said that's how it sounded.' He looked at her sombrely. 'Just tell me this. Have you read or heard anywhere else of Jerry's shunting not just the poor sods with two good legs, but their sick, on this damned march?'

'No, but I hardly ever see the papers these days or hear the BBC news, Why bother? News is always days late.'

'Isn't that a fact? Remember last month? Monty's lot crossed the Rhine on a Friday and it was not till Monday morning that *The Times* and others broke it to the poor damned British public. Mother of God, whose bloody war do they think this is?'

Sarah shrugged and didn't remind him of the innumerable times he had told her this war was none of his bloody business. He's changed, she thought, I'm not sure if he knows it, but he has. Not changed sides; just changed.

'And what more do you suppose is still under the covers waiting for someone to stumble over?'

She quoted Dacey. 'Not knowing, can't say,' and they went their separate ways in mutual ignorance in this context as neither had seen, nor heard mentioned even by Dacey, one particular small column in some of yesterday's papers.

That particular news published the previous day, Saturday 14th April, was unusual, as it reported a unique twelve-hour truce between the British and German Armies in the immediate area of what was named by the Germans as Belsen Internment Camp, that had resulted in the British taking over the guarding of the camp at the request of the Germans, as typhus was rampant. The negotiations for this truce had involved ringing Himmler, who could not be reached; his Chief-of-Staff had spoken for him and rejected the proposal, but, nevertheless, it had been confirmed between the parties on the ground and confirmed to the area around Winsen Bridge. After the British Army had taken over the camp the German guards were allowed to withdraw to their own lines and the Germans than blew up Winsen Bridge.

It was not until Thursday, 19th April, 1945, that the British newspapers first published the photographs and reports that stunned the British and world public with initially incredulous horror. The photographs were of the corpses and living victims from the German cencentration camps at Ohrdruf, Nordhausen and Buchenwald. Amongst those reports was the first upon Belsen that was issued by the British 2nd Army's Headquarters on 18th April and included a verbal account of a very senior Medical Officer who had just spent forty-eight hours in the camp. He was reported as describing the place as the most horrible, frightful, he had ever seen and where the corpses had been left lying in great unburied heaps, or packed amongst the living sick; the starvation and cannibalism had been worse than the typhus; and the British guards had had to fire over the prisoner's heads to keep them away from the food stores the British had brought in, and, initially, had to guard those stores with tanks.

One afternoon in Alex a few days later, when Sister was off two-to-five, the unexpected appearance in the flat of Nigel Hastings and Dick Dunlop, swaggering in patently new khaki battledresses, drew Sarah from the desk, Nurse Yates from stock-making in the duty-room and Nurse Burton from preparing teas in the kitchen. 'What on earth are you two doing back in London all dressed up as soldiers?' Nurse Burton demanded in the voice of a prefect discovering a fourth-former wearing hockey boots in assembly hall.

'Just looked in to say hail and farewell, nurses,' said Nigel Hastings, beaming with pride.

Dick Dunlop added, 'Seems the Army, the British Red Cross, the St John's Ambulance and such chaps, need stout-hearted chaps to help them with this and that over the water, and as none come more stout-hearted than

Martha's student men, ten of our year are off this evening.'

The three nurses exchanged identical glances. Sarah asked, 'Just Martha's men?'

'Not so. Teaching hospitals all over London are shelling out final-year student men. According to gen – about ninety of us.'

Nurse Yates frowned. 'Know where you're going?'

'Come, come, nurse, careless talk costs lives! We know. We've read the posters.'

'Huh! I hope you've had anti-typhus shots.'

'Shots, Nurse Yates? We are human pin-cushions. And how's dear old Alex, Nurse Thane?'

'Ticking nicely, thanks.'

'Carry on ticking whilst we just nip over to finish off the job for Ike! See you around, nurses. Think of us tenderly when we are gone. Cheers!'

'Cheers,' echoed the nurses watching the students swagger back into the ground-floor corridor.

Nurse Yates, still frowning, muttered, 'I'll bet the lucky things end up in Belsen. Why send students that know nothing about actually nursing the sick and not us!'

Sarah said unemotionally. 'The students are men of military age and, academically, they know quite a bit. Anyway, we're civvy nurses and needed here even if, according to Mr Ernest Bevin, we're not doing National Service, but he's working on that one.' She looked at her juniors' amazed faces. 'I kid you not. Most of my set have now had his official bumf saying that as SRNs they can't finish their fourth year and must leave for either midder or TB courses. I haven't had my bumf and I suspect only as Matron's pulled a string to keep me reserved because Alex's permanent staff nurse still can't leave her mother.'

The new indignation had driven the students and their possible destination from Nurse Yate's mind. 'You're telling us doing a civvy general training isn't National Service, nurse?'

'As I've just said, not according to our present Minister of Labour. Don't take my word for it. Just nip up to the Home's top corridor and take a look at the official notice about this that ends with Ernie Bevin's printed signature. Senior Sister Tutor pinned it up on our notice board, grinding her teeth on our behalf.'

For once, Nurse Yates was speechless.

Not Nurse Burton. 'I say, nurse! This is the giddy limit! Aren't you fourth-years livid?'

Sarah had forgotten neither the students nor recent newspaper photographs. 'It hasn't exactly made Ernie Bevin our pin-up, but as this country's apparently run out of pupil-midwives and TB nurses, presumably he's got to nab all the new SRNs in civvy street he can lay hands on.'

'But to say the work you've been doing all war wasn't National Service – '

'Could have put it more tactfully,' allowed Sarah, before returning to the desk to wonder unhappily over the students' next and Charles's present destination and whether there was any limit to man's inhumanity to man.

Three days later she had the answer to all three. The answer to her final question was – no.

Those answers came in Charles's third letter that was dated '21/4/45', written from his new billet in the clean, well-appointed barrack blocks that had until the last two weeks housed a German Panzer Training School and German Army Hospital, and stood just outside the gates of Belsen camp. As before, the letter was written on RAMC case history sheets, but on this occasion in the dreadful anger of a peaceful man finally aroused to white-hot fury.

My unit got here seven days ago, a few hours after our troops first opened it up. That day back at 'dispersal', there was an 'all RAMC personnel, all regimental stretcher-bearers, to Company office on the double.' None of us knew why, where we were going, or what to

154

expect till we got here. Here — is called BELSEN — but, Christ — that isn't the name — there isn't one sufficiently bloody to fit. The Germans rated it a SICK CAMP — i.e. for poor devils of slave-labourers too ill to work. Sick? Bloody hell. I have seen nothing, I repeat NOTHING to show that the starving, living skeletons we've found here had any kind of medical treatment — but, yes, they've had treatment — get this! No beds, bedding, bedclothes. Some do have torn, filthy, blue-and-white striped sort of pyjamas or gowns, but whether clothed, naked, sick, dying or dead the lot — the lot — are coated in old faeces. Their beds are either wire or wooden three-tiered bunks jammed against the sides of huts roughly 100 foot long, 30 wide, with the living using the rotting bodies of the dead for warmth. I can't describe the smell in the huts or over the whole camp but, after it, hell itself must smell clean and here's just one reason why:

When we got here the mounds of the unburied dead were higher than Block 7 before being sliced and other bodies were layered in open ditches bigger than H.E. craters — just lying there, men, women, kids, babies — 12,000 corpses — yes, twelve thousand unburied. I saw them. *SAW*.

We're still losing hundreds daily. The whole camp's alive (wrong word but has to serve) with TB, typhus, typhoid, dysentery, pellagra, lice, gangrene, scabies — and the sheer, nightmarish hell in every survivor's face. How could the Germans do this? (I don't say 'Jerry' as I have shed that specific syndrome.) One of our first troops in told me when he took over from a German guard, the bastard said, 'You will observe here we have no gas chambers.' Had I been there I'd have said, 'Why waste good gas when the bugs have done the job for you?' but just as well I wasn't as I'd probably have killed him with my hands. I never thought I could or would ever want to kill, but I was wrong. I haven't come across one of our chaps here who doesn't feel the same or right now would give a damn if we had to start fighting the Germans again from square one.

I've heard a body of med. students that includes Martha's men are coming out from England. Not come yet, but we can use them.

Sarah, I'm sorry to write all this, but I must to hang on to sanity. This place isn't only hideous, sickening and agonising, it's evil. Calculated evil. I've heard the British – and I think Yank – press have been here taking photos, so imagine you've already some idea of what it's like. Only some. Photos you can't smell or hear – and some sounds can't be recognised when heard. Tell you why – when my Cpl and I went into our first hut after arrival and stood for a few seconds in dumb horror, suddenly there was a quite hellish, thin, high-pitched wailing from both sides that froze the soul and we took for wails of pain. Then a Polish chap that spoke some English grabbed at my knees – he was too weak to get off the floor – and said, 'They are cheering you, Herr Englisch Doktor.'

Despite the daily death-rate, things are moving fast. We're evacuating as many as we can, fast, saving some of the others, not all. Once we've got them all out our flame-throwers will burn the whole camp to the ground, but none of us'll forget how it looked, nor should we. If anyone ever wants to know why we'd to fight this war, I've a one-word answer – BELSEN.

Forgive my writing this – but I know you will or I wouldn't have been able to write it. (Probably the censor'll cut it to ribbons, anyway).

I hope you are well and safe.

Yours,

Charles.

That letter reached Sarah stamped as passed by the censor, and unaltered. She read it alone in her room, and then needed three cigarettes before she could re-read it. And when she had replaced it in its envelope she lay flat on her bed with her eyes closed and forgetting she still wore a cap. It was a long time before she re-opened her eyes and during that time her mental vision functioned like an over-speeded film projector throwing images of faces onto a camera screen.

Faces of friends she had liked; faces of casual wartime acquaintances she would have liked had she had time to know them better; faces of patients she had liked, and often, loved; faces of her dead brother, of the dead sailor she had loved, of the UNKNOWN little girl she had watched die in Alex on the evening of M-Day. And as she had watched all those faces behind her closed eyes, she had remembered how often she had thought – as millions of others must have thought – why? WHY? Surely, nothing justifies this and there must have been some other way to settle things without a war.

No, she thought now, lying with her eyes open, no. There was no other way. Evil's like carcinoma. Once either have taken root, the only way to stop it is to cut it out; trying to pretend it doesn't exist won't make it go away; on the contrary, it'll continue to grow until the whole body is diseased and by then there's nothing anyone can do to stop it. This evil had to be stopped and cut out by war and war, like surgery, when cutting out diseased tissue has to destroy some that's healthy.

'Some', her mind echoed and she winced physically at that dreadful understatement. Millions of lives lost, millions of living lives wrecked, she thought, that's what this war has cost and I've only seen a minute fraction of that cost. But even the most terrible things that I've seen happen to people, or that had happened before I saw them, had one good common factor. All I saw were in this country

157

where, always, everyone – in and out of hospital – wanted to help them and mourned, if only briefly, very genuinely, those beyond their help.

Another echo, 'How could the Germans do it?' and with it the total recognition of Charles's implacable 'I don't say "Jerry" as I have shed that specific syndrome.' And so have I thought Sarah, and so have I. 'Jerry', the good fighting man, was a chap I've often feared, never hated, and always respected.

Respected? She raised herself on one elbow and looked at the large buff envelope on her bedtable and there was an expression on her face that had never been there before and made her look older, hard, and dangerous with the anger now consuming her as a nurse as well as a human being, just as it had Charles as a doctor, it was directed at those that could willingly, knowingly, mistreat the sick and injured. And, being a child of her generation, she thought, aloud in the words of her generation. 'Tell that one to the Marines,' said Sarah to her room in an icy and implacable anger.

On leaving Alex to the night staff, Sarah decided to go out through Casualty in the hope that Dacey had some peace gen. Sister Casualty had gone off-duty at six, it was now nearly half-past nine, but only for the last few minutes had Casualty Hall been empty of patients for the first time since nine this morning. The newest dressers, in limp shirtsleeves with limp masks round their throats, were slumped in the wheelchairs lined against the wall opposite the lodge. Dacey had come out for air and was propped against the closed half of the stable door. Paddy and Mr Lawson lounged on the nearest bench, the two night juniors were invisible, and the night senior, one of Nurse Mayhew's set, stood yawning in the nearest open doorway. At Sarah's approach she called 'No. Not come yet, nurse. But London's decided the war's over.'

'Mother of God, but that's a fact.' Paddy rose wearily. 'Hordes in all day. "Just thought I'd step in with me old trouble in the back seeing you'll be nice and quiet, doctor." Give me damned strength! Old troubles in the back — new troubles in the throats — cruel headaches — gastric stomachs playing up shocking — sure as hell if I've to palpate one more gastric stomach this day my gastric stomach'll play up more than shocking — it'll throw up no less!'

Sarah smiled sympathetically, the night senior stifled another yawn, and Mr Lawson, too tired to smile or stand, queried mildly, 'Needing treatment for writer's cramp, Dacey?'

'Small wonder if I do, Mr Lawson.' Dacey, spruce, greying and sturdy, paused to ensure full attention. 'Sister Cas. asked me to do some totting up seeing we closed the book, Nurse Thane. How many would you reckon the doodles and rockets fetched in here', he jerked a thumb at the gap between the blast and sandbag walls, 'from second week last June to third this March? In all, mind. Majors, minors, BIDs [Brought In Dead]. Give it a try?'

The dressers looked bored. They had missed all the fun and were up to the back teeth with 'you chaps/boys/young gentlemen don't know your luck.'

Sarah said, 'Sorry, Dacey. Not knowing, can't say.'

Dacey chuckled. He enjoyed being an hospital legend in his own lifetime. 'Two short of thirty thousand. Just the one hospital. Makes you think.'

The dressers exchanged bored glances, Paddy and the nurses glances of another nature, and Mr Lawson blinked through his moon glasses at no one in particular. 'Wasn't counting,' he apologised.

'We'll forgive you, Tom. Just the once,' said Paddy. 'Off for a good lie-in in the morning, Nurse Thane?'

Sarah shook her head, knowing why he had asked, and that she was about to make his night. 'No, Dr Brown. Unlike some wards that are splitting tomorrow, Sister Alex

is giving us proper Victory half-days and, like you residents, we drew lots. Yates, Burton and I've drawn
tomorrow, Sister, Martin and Grey, Wednesday.'

Paddy's tired eyes brightened. 'Tom's tomorrow. I'm
Wednesday. Let us now hope Ike plays ball.' He waved his
long thin arms. 'Talk about where we came in. Kicked-off
with a phoney war and right now the referee's swallowed
his whistle and here we are in a phoney peace waiting for
the bug – my apologies, nurse! – waiting for the gallant
warrior to blow end of injury time, period.'

'In that case I'm off to a bath and bed.' Sarah waved a
general goodnight and strolled on into the darkening Yard.

'I could use some air.' Paddy ambled after her and when
beyond the gap called softly, 'A word in your shell-like,
Sarah.'

She stopped in the shelter of a blast wall. 'What's on
your mind, Paddy?'

'You know damn well. Val Martin nipping home,
Wednesday?'

'No. Too much of a sweat going up and down in a half-
day even without the trains being as packed as they're
bound to be if Ike does his stuff.' She looked around at the
deepening shadows of the standing blocks, guarding walls,
rubble mounds and parked ambulances, and then at the
traffic that was no heavier nor lighter than usual in the road
running past the hospital. 'Phoney peace, is how it looks.'

'That's for sure.' He dug his hands in his limp white coat
pockets. 'No one's having to burst out singing this time
round, but could happen yet. How is she?'

Sarah thought before answering, but knew that whatever she said would not affect the immediate outcome.
Inevitable, she mused. He's fallen for Val and had his
interest sharpened by her long unavailability, he's Val's
type and, above all, around. It could be disastrous for both
if he could afford a wife and Val didn't have to start midder
in August – and not only because both need shoulders in

moments of crisis. He's far too bright for Val, and once he's got used to looking at her she'll bore him stiff; though she's sweet and kind, she'll never be able to handle his volatile temperament or intelligence. She said at last, 'Bit down but bearing up. Wanting to date her Wednesday?'

'Think I could?' She nodded. 'You're a lovely girl, Sarah! Should I ring her tonight?'

Charles wouldn't have asked that of anyone, thought Sarah. She said, 'Yes. Not too late.'

'May all the angels bless you.' He shot back into Casualty, his long white coat flapping.

Sarah walked on, wondering absently why he hadn't asked what colour tie he should wear on Wednesday afternoon, and then pondering on the saying that the world was divided into the borrowers and the lenders. From there, as constantly recently, her mind drifted to Charles and how their relationship had altered – as such relationships invariably did – after his telling her that he loved and wanted to marry her. Altered still more, she reflected, by his letters. He's a rather wonderful man, but I don't want to marry him – marry anyone – until this uncertain peace is certain all over the world, and even then, no hurry for a life-long tie after years of being tied. Nearly six years – and the war's had our whole generation by the throat – wear this uniform – go here – there – do this – do that – put up with whatever – no say from the individual ever and, whatever Ike says tonight, still no say for the Armed Forces or single, civvy, newly trained nurses. Like Paddy said – this is where we came in. . . .

After her bath, Sarah opened her curtains, hesitated, then took down the blackout screen, pushed up the bottom sash of the window and climbed out in dressing gown and pyjamas, leaving on the light. All the other top-floor rooms were blacked out and the light from Sarah's hit the concrete like a searchlight. She leaned on the parapet that faced the hospital and looked across at the now black,

161

angular outlines of the standing blocks and down at the now invisible blast and sandbag walls backing Casualty Yard, and the red hurricane lamps put out nightly to guide in-coming ambulances, glowed like lighted cigar ends. All around, on both sides of the river, the blackouts were still up, the streets still black caverns, and the traffic still crawled behind slits in blackened headlights. But on the southern side just a few bonfires had been lit on old bombsites and made disturbingly reminiscent crimson patches in the darkness, and the handful of fireworks which suddenly exploded in a neighbouring side street were too similar to gunfire for enjoyment.

London's not all lit-up yet, thought Sarah. London's learnt to take good news with a bucket of salt until established beyond doubt. And then the sounding of a tug's hooter that in seconds was joined by those of other tugs and the sirens of the ships in the docks, tingled the back of her neck.

'Hey, girls!' She shouted to the darkened top-floor windows. 'Has it come?'

A cheerful voice shouted back, 'Not yet. I've got my wireless on. Those ships should take more water with it. Ike's obviously gone to sleep.'

A second, irate voice bellowed, 'I wish you two and those ruddy ships would realise some of us are trying to sleep!'

Sarah yelled, 'Sorry, Pam!' and smiling a little to herself, she glanced upwards and noticed the sky was heavy with thunder clouds. Pam's had it, she thought, climbing back into her room and leaving down the blackout screen.

The thunder started before she fell asleep on her stomach with her right cheek pressed into and not under her two pillows. It was a violent storm and her last waking thought was, Acts of God may awe me, but it's the acts of man that bloody terrify me. She was fast asleep when the storm faded and the war with Germany was officially ended. At two minutes after that midnight, General Eisenhower issued the public announcement that he had accepted Germany's unconditional surrender and that all hostilities in Europe had ceased.

CHAPTER TEN

'CAN'T say it won't make a nice change, Nurse Thane,' said the Alex patients at seven-thirty in the morning, 'and must say it's a real treat to know there'll be no more bombs, rockets and nasty doodlebugs. Going to take a bit of getting used to, mind.'

Nurse Mayhew confided wearily, 'I put it in my written report, Nurse Thane. You feel victorious?' Sarah shook her bemused head. 'Nor me.'

At ten minutes to eight Sister Alex came on-duty carrying a great bunch of golden forsythia that she had just bought from one of the elderly flower-women already installed with their baskets on the pavements on either side of the gateless entrance to Casualty Yard, as on all weekend afternoons, Bank Holidays and the King's birthday. 'Soon as I saw them from my window, I knew Ike had spoken before I turned on my wireless. And as today's our first public holiday to celebrate what everyone seems to be calling VE and we've no flags or buntings to decorate the ward, I thought Alex should have the extra bit of jollity.'

'Sister, what a lovely idea. They're glorious,' said Sarah, shamed by Sister's smiling serenity into copying her attitude and consciously stifling her desolation that neither her father, brother, nor the man she had once loved, could see today. Not that they ever doubted today would come, she thought, and now I think of it, nor did I. I was always sure we'd win, even although looking back – sometimes, God only knows how or why – but I was sure. In fact, it's the only thing about which I've been sure since the war started.

After prayers and the general enthusiasm for the forsythia on the desk, the patients first voiced the question that was to be repeated all round the hospital all morning. 'When are THEY turning on the lights?'

Nurse Yates, being off today, just knew it wouldn't be before tomorrow night. Nurse Burton couldn't see why the chaps with their fuse-wires and whatnots couldn't get them on by tonight. Daisy, primed by the Repairs and Works mechanic she had met when returning the empty electric food trolley to the main kitchen after breakfast, reckoned not a chance before tomorrow seeing all over London there'd be old bulbs, fuses and cables needing more than a mite of seeing to. Then, having drawn today in the wardmaids' lottery, she retreated to her kitchen to spend the morning singing 'Don't Fence Me In'.

Sister said, 'I'm sure it'll be tonight. It won't be really dark till after ten, Thane. That'll give the electricians time.'

'It is a public holiday, Sister.'

'I don't think that'll stop them.' She looked around the tidy ward awaiting the first residents' rounds. 'What are you doing with your VE hols?'

'Four of my set have asked me to go across the river and join the party, Sister,' said Sarah truthfully, but not adding the further truth that she had refused the invitation on the acceptable grounds that she had letters to write, was too small to see anything but backs of heads in any crowd and could see all she wanted from the Home's roof-garden. She liked and got along well with her own sex, but all-girls-together outings had never appealed to her, and she had always preferred her own to indifferent company of either sex, especially upon special occasions. Were Charles here, she thought suddenly, then doused the thought. He's not. Skip it.

Sister Alex knew her better than Sarah realised. 'I suspect parties will be breaking out all over. Matron's giving a Sisters' coffee party after the day staff come off tonight and if they do turn on the lights I know that we — and I'll bet everyone here who can make it and hasn't already crossed the river — will be out on the terrace to watch. If you're back and at a loose end, don't watch alone. Come and join us.'

Sarah's admiration for Sister rose to a new peak. 'Thanks a lot, Sister. May I take a raincheck?' she added, then promptly wished she had used another cliché.

'Please! Ah — here come the men.'

Dr Roberts and Paddy came in smiling, and wearing button-holes of scarlet carnations safety-pinned to their white coat lapels. 'Courtesy of Professor Medicine, Sister,' said the SMO. 'You will note even Dr Brown has succumbed. Can it be he's forgiven us for Cromwell?'

'Perish the thought, Sister! But where's the Irishman that didn't enjoy a good party? And have you heard of the latest party in Cas.? Early this morning the dressers festooned the joint with old bunting from King George and Queen Mary's Silver Jubilee that Dacey disinterred from somewhere and Sister Cas's now insisting the lot comes down stat as she's running a Casualty Department and not a jamboree in Piccadilly Circus!'

Sister laughed and the patients, without hearing the joke, laughed with her. And Sarah, standing by the desk smiling professionally, thought, it is sinking into the patients and I'm happy for them, but I can't yet feel anything for me. Why not? Because I still can't believe it? Probably.

Sister Alex was saying, 'War or peace, Dr Brown, Sister Cas. is Sister Cas.'

'That's a fact, Sister.' Paddy caught Sarah's eye and surreptitiously crossed himself.

It was a few minutes to one and Sister had just returned from second lunch to free Sarah at one and already dismissed Nurse Yates and Burton, when Dacey rang Alex.

'You take it, Thane. I must shoo off Daisy.'

'Dacey here, Nurse Thane. London's lights being turned on ten-thirty tonight, official.'

Momentarily, Sarah couldn't answer. It's true – it – is – true. Thank God. 'Oh – er – thanks, Dacey.'

'No trouble, nurse.' From his voice he was smiling. 'Don't take any wooden tanners, mind.' He rang off.

Sister had just re-appeared with Daisy and Sarah handed on the news, when the telephone rang again, 'Mine, Nurse Thane! You're off – Sister Alexandra speaking – oh, good afternoon, Professor!' Sister listened, beckoned Sarah eagerly, said into the receiver, 'Here with me now, Professor – ' then handed it to Sarah. 'Professor Pathology would like a word, Nurse Thane,' she said dead-pan.

Sarah was too startled to think. She stared wide-eyed at Sister and took the receiver. 'Nurse Thane speaking. Good afternoon, Professor – '

'A very good afternoon to you, Nurse Thane. Am I rightly informed that you are off-duty and about to go to lunch? I am ? Splendid. In the light of the general consensus that small celebrations are in order, Sister Dining-Room – I hasten to add with Matron's approval – has kindly permitted some of my chaps to collect the necessary for the small gathering I'm holding in the pathologists' common room. Two doors on from the In-Patients Lab., but you'll know it – and I would be honoured if you would care to join us.'

Sarah had to swallow.' Thank you very much, Professor. Er – now?'

'Just so, nurse. Just so. Come straight up. One of my chaps will be looking out for you.'

Sarah put down. 'Sister, he's throwing a party and has asked me up.'

'Very nice too. I said parties would be breaking out all over. Hang on a tick for me.' Sister ducked into the dutyroom and ducked back with a small bottle of cough

167

lozenges. 'Take these. Smell to high heaven of peppermint. If you spot Matron, the Assistant Matron or an Office Sister when leaving the party, suck one, stat. Off you go and enjoy yourself.'

She's marvellous, everyone's marvellous, but me, thought Sarah, leaving Alex a few minutes later in her clean spare apron, with her hair newly combed and face newly powdered. I am genuinely thankful for everything, but I'm just not in party mood. She walked quickly along the ground-floor corridor, looking at the floor ahead, so it was not until she turned into Central Hall that she saw Charles waiting for her at the foot of the marble, un-carpeted front stairs.

Charles, in battledress and bareheaded, stood facing the lighted corridor. Aside from the missing long white coat and wooden box under one arm, he looked to Sarah's astounded first glance exactly as upon their encounters around the hospital when he had been postgradding, and that was as if he had just had a wash, shave and brush-up and was mildly pleased to see her but didn't expect her to remember his name. The second glance that she needed to believe the evidence of her eyes showed her that he looked older, and that his face was thinner and there was about him an air of inexpressive weariness that was unrelated to anything as simple as physiological fatigue. Her mind flashed with the thought: before, only his body was wounded.

He raised his right hand in silent welcome as they moved slowly towards each other. She looked up at him and said quietly, 'Charles, I'm so glad you're here. How? And how long've you got?'

On seeing her expression when she first saw him he had felt his pulse-rate shoot up to around 132. Her greeting didn't lower it. He answered her in reverse, and carefully. 'What's left of a twenty-four. Fly back tomorrow morning. I got flown over early this morning to take one of our chaps

168

to East Grinstead.' He saw she had immediately appreciated the significance of his escorting mission to arguably the most deservedly renowned Plastic Surgery Unit in the UK, and that it was one he could not yet tolerate enlarging upon. He went on, 'After handing him over I tried to ring Martha's from the hospital, but all trunk lines to London were busy or booked solid for hours. Then I struck lucky. An RAF ambulance taking two chaps to St George's let me hitch a lift up.' They had begun slowly ascending the stairs and suddenly his voice lightened. 'We'd the hell of a job getting through to Knightsbridge even from the West. I walked, or rather, shoved the rest. Not even a panzer division would now get through Central London. Crowds are milling all over the roads and, far as I could make out, all traffic's stopped from Hyde Park Corner to Westminster. Whether cops or crowds first stopped the traffic, I wouldn't know, but my money's on the crowds. When I got here Dacey said you were on-duty till one so I went up to the In-Patients Lab to look in on the chaps and was roped-in stat by the old man who's in tremendous form and asked what the devil I thought I was doing showing up at his get-together without – quote – that pretty little Nurse Whatsit in Whosit with the most beautiful eyes he'd seen in a woman for more years than he cared to recall – unquote, and then got on the phone to corral you. Okay by you?'

'Okay?' They had reached the first-floor landing and she stopped to smile at him and polish the nails of her right hand on her clean apron bib. 'Biggest social boost of my Martha's life. First time a pundit's asked me to his party. Just one of the chosen elite, that's me. Thanks a lot, Charles.' Suddenly, she was grave. 'I was wishing you could be here today. I wish it could have been – something else – that got you back, but I'm so glad you're here.'

'Snap, on all counts,' he muttered, as he needed all his self-control not to lift her up and kiss her. As she was in uniform and in the hospital, it was fortunate for their future careers that he kept control. A door had opened and onto the landing had come Miss Elwes, the Office Sister who had relieved Sister Alex's compassionate leave, and Professor Pathology. Both held small tumblers half-filled with beer, and in the Professor's free hand was a lighted cigarette and his habitual spare was tucked above his right ear.

'Ah! There you are! About to send out search parties! Come along in, Nurse Thane – Sister, of course, you know well – Sister, I believe you know Dr Bradley – of course, of course, now then, Nurse Thane, what's your tipple? I can offer you beer, beer, beer, or beer? Shocking state of affairs! Win a war and not a drop of gin to be had in Martha's nor, they tell me, all London. Even the hard stuff under the counter's run dry – beer's running out so fast hardly be a drop left to toast the lights. Not to worry! We haven't run out yet – come along, come along! I've saved each of you a spam sandwich,' continued the Professor, whilst simultaneously beaming, smoking and waving his beer tumbler. 'We have other varieties, but what they purport to contain I have deemed it more prudent not to analyse, but as we've won a war Sister Dining-Room has risen to the occasion and provided us with one spam sandwich per head – this way, ladies, this way. . . .'

Big Ben was striking six when Charles and Sarah joined the human avalanche still flowing westwards over Westminster Bridge. Sarah had changed into her purple blouse and black corduroy jacket and skirt, and wore lipstick and small, plain silver clip-on earrings and an intangible glow that was a combination of wonder, relief, happiness and youth. That combination had worked the same magic upon Charles, tightly holding Sarah's hand. He felt the crowd pressing them closer and infecting them with the universal happiness to add to their own. The hair under his beret was

170

still wet from being held under one of the Lab's elbow taps after Sarah had left the Professor's private office to get changed. 'Give me twenty minutes, Charles. Okay?'

'Couldn't be better.' He touched his face. 'Time for a shave.'

The Professor had swept both into his office when the party broke up shortly after four o'clock. 'I need one of those coffees the chap has just brought up from the canteen, Bradley. Grab three mugs and bring 'em in here. Dislike drinking cuppas alone – bad habit, drinking alone. Armchair for you, nurse! I'll have my own and Bradley can use the spare – that's the form, Bradley, hand 'em round – no, leave mine on the desk – just recollect a matter I must mention to Dr Anthony – ' and he swept out closing the door.

Charles looked from the door to Sarah. 'Dacey must look to his laurels.'

'Yes.' She had to look away, so she looked around the smallish, window-bricked riverside office that had two wooden walls. 'I've always thought Prof. Path a poppet. Now my pin-up pundit.'

'He'll like that.'

She looked at him. He was sipping coffee perched on one edge of the desk, and looking younger and much less weary than a few hours ago and she sensed that more for her, and others, than himself, he had battened the mental shutters. 'He likes you a lot, Charles. Has he offered you a path. job when the lot's over?'

'Mentioned it.' He put down the mug to light a cigarette. 'Sorry I can't offer you one.'

She shrugged smiling. 'Half a tooth tumbler of flat beer in uniform on VE, yes. A fag, no. I won't need these.' She showed him the cough lozenges, and they both laughed, as the youth they had had to ignore for so long was surging within them. 'Think you'd like to take up the Prof.'s offer?'

He nodded. 'I used to think my line was general

171

medicine, but in my stint up here I got rather hooked on pathology – inter alia.' Sarah's faint blush again dramatically raised his pulse-rate. He went on a little breathlessly, 'When the Jap show's over there'll be queues of chaps for every medical job going in the UK, so I'm damned lucky to have got a foot in early and the chance of working under as decent a boss as I could wish for. In any joint, it's the boss that makes or buggers-up – oh, sorry – that messes-up the show.' His mouth had tightened briefly as the mental shutters had jerked open and taken his mind back to this time yesterday and where he must be this time tomorrow.

Sarah, watching, read his mind, and knowing the value of counter-irritants, she said quickly, 'I've just remembered his youngest son was in the 8th Army. That isn't only why he likes you, or why I do, but when we first met, it helped more than it hurt. I never knew either of his sons but I've always heard they were nice.'

He looked at her gratefully. 'Same here. Very decent chaps. Like their father.'

'Do you resemble your father? You've never said.'

He moved off the desk and stood looking down at her, his hands in his trouser pockets. 'My dear girl, there is so much I haven't said to you, or you to me, that it could be said we actually know damn-all about each other. I don't go along with that.' He paused and she kept silent, knowing he hadn't finished. He reached to put out the cigarette he had left burning in an ashtray and lit another before he spoke again. Then, 'My father was in the ICS [Indian Civil Service]. He died in India – cholera – in '37, a few months after my mother – septicaemia after a scratch on her wrist.'

'Oh, Charles – '

'No.' He was quick. 'Yes, it was tough but not as tough as it could have been as I never knew my parents very well. It wasn't their fault. They had to send me back to a school in England when I was seven and after that I only saw them on father's leaves every three or five years. Father's only brother was my legal guardian in this country. He was damned good to me. He was a widower, no kids, always wanted them, so I got the benefit.' He thought a few moments. 'Yes. My uncle used to say I reminded him quite a bit of my father – same build – hair – that sort of thing.'

'Your mother fair?' she asked, thinking how right he was about their knowing so little, and yet so much, about each other.

'Yes.' He smiled reminiscently and his smile was deeply affectionate and had a hint of pride that touched her heart for him. 'She was extremely pretty. Very similar looks to your pal Val.' He turned to stub his half-smoked cigarette. 'How is Val?'

She told him the truth as she saw it.

He nodded. 'Yes. I'll go along with that. She's always struck me as a sweet, but incredibly immature kid. Pro tem, for her sake, as well. May I ask you something?'

'Go ahead.'

'How come you and she are such pals? You're such different types?'

She had to think. 'I'm not sure. We just hit it off in the PTS [Preliminary Training School], I'm not sure why – yes, I am. Charles, she was so damned helpless. She was nineteen and had never even cut her own finger-nails. Mummy had always done it and as she was a day-boarder in a convent, Mummy was there every night. Someone had to teach her a few elementary facts of life and I took on the job because I liked her, was sorry for her – and probably because being the Oracle of the PTS boosted my own ego. I needed that after suddenly finding myself in an all-female environment. I was used to that at school, but then father and David balanced things up in the holidays. Only hols Martha's first-years get is one week after PTS ends and then three when the year ends. Make sense?'

'Very much so. My own set-up was so all-male that

173

David had to do a you-on-Val, on me at Cambridge. He wasn't a bad tutor, but even so, nurses still scared the hell out of me when I was first a student. I knew what to do with girls but not what to say to them.' He laughed suddenly. 'I can hear David's "For Christ sake, tell 'em they're different and that's what you like about them — works every time." Never did for me, but that didn't stop him.' Again he paused and she was silent. 'He was a damned good chap, Sarah, and you two had so much in common that I know you must've had a very fine father. And you know I mean that.'

Her eyes were luminous with unshed tears and met his own. 'Yes. I know. And, yes, we did. And — thank you.'

He inclined his head and for a little looked at her in silence. 'When I first got to Germany last month,' he said almost conversationally, 'I remembered your saying, one night having supper after the theatre, how, after this war started, your father started talking to you about the last show. My father was in that war, but the only time he ever mentioned it to my hearing was when we took a long walk together on his last leave home. I was — what? — sixteen. He suddenly opened up. I didn't know why then but, with hindsight, I'd say he knew this one was coming and I'd be involved and wanted to dry some of the wetness behind my ears before the balloon went up. He talked quite a bit on that walk and one thing he said I remembered in Germany. He said that not once in his war had he been able to talk of it on leave at home, and I said, "Not even to mother?" and he said, "Good God, no, boy! Never."' He lit another cigarette and inhaled deeply. 'I only properly understood his attitude after I got caught up in our war and, until I met you, Sarah — ' he shook his head ' — nobody. But to you, when I'm away from you, I can talk on paper, and when with you — I think — I can talk without words. Am I right?'

'Yes. At least, I think so too,' was all she had time to say before Professor Pathology, Dr Anthony and another pathologist came in together and the conversation became general.

They had initially planned a round trip of Whitehall, Trafalgar Square, The Mall, Buckingham Palace, Buckingham Gate, Birdcage Walk that would return them to Parliament Square in time for supper, and any drinks going, in a small underground restaurant in a side street just behind the Westminster corner of Whitehall. They kept to that itinerary, but had agreed to miss supper before they reached Trafalgar Square, to the general approval of their very near neighbours. 'If you could get the seat, won't be worth the five bob a head give or take the cover charge, mate, not tonight it won't – kitchen staff be bunging anything on plates to get done sharpish and out to take a butcher's at the lights – and they was saying back of this lot as there's not an unbooked seat to be had in the one restaurant or caffy round here and pubs having to bung up their shutters sharpish after opening as they've run dry, seemingly. Talk about getting all lit up – when the lights come on! Chance'd be a fine thing – got to laugh!'

The laughter was as omnipresent as the cheering and the outbursts of singing, and all three rolled in waves over the crowds covering roads, pavements, traffic islands, lampposts and every available ledge. Wave after wave, and each wave gathering others as it rolled on; between the waves, euphoric greetings to and from total strangers, swopping of brief war histories as old war jokes all had heard interminably and received as if newly minted by Tommy Handley, Vic Oliver, Bebe Daniels, Ben Lyon, Arthur Askey, Kenneth Horne, Richard Murdoch and other comics of beloved wartime wireless fame, or by London's especially beloved Max Miller and the great Sid Field whose genius had filled the Prince of Wales Theatre with unstoppable laughter in times when London had desperately needed to laugh. And intermingled with the exchanges and cheers, the songs — 'Roll Out The Barrel' — inevitably followed by euphorically self-derisive cheers — 'Knock 'em In The Old Kent Road', 'The Lambeth Walk', 'My Old Dutch', 'Knees Up Mother Brown' — even when there was no space for raising a single knee — and any other old or new popular song that a few voices started and was immediately taken up by thousands of others. Thousands in assorted Allied uniforms; hundreds of thousands in war-shabby civilian clothes; both sexes, all ages, all shapes, and all smiling.

When they reached Trafalgar Square there was briefly just enough room for dancing. They were swept, clinging together, into one of the gigantic lines doing the Palais Glide that continued into the Hokey-Cokey until the pressure of the surrounding crowd rendered impossible putting the left foot out and shaking anything all about and the lines disintegrated to a hurricane of applause.

Charles, laughing, lifted Sarah to his own face level. 'When the old lady goes to town she don't need a drop too much!'

She hugged him for voicing her thoughts and for the joy of being able to share them with him. 'I was just thinking London's dusted down and donned her best bonnet, picked up her skirts and is shaking a leg — and my God, Charles, hasn't she earned this!'

He didn't answer with words. His arms tightened as he looked for a few moments into her eyes and then he kissed her lips for the first time. He did not kiss her quite as he had longed to from their first meeting, but, even so, it made him feel as if his bones had turned to water. When she kissed him back as gently, he very nearly dropped her.

They were in The Mall when he bent his knees as his only means of lowering himself to shout, 'Here he comes again, Sarah!' before again lifting her to his level but this time with her back to him and in what had become their established procedure, she steadying herself with one arm round the back of his neck. Above the heads in front they saw two policemen coaxing the crowds temporarily aside to let through the Prime Minister's official black car at walking pace. It was the fourth time they had seen this since crossing Westminster Bridge and, as before, Mr Churchill sat alone in the back, beaming and waving through clouds of cigar smoke, a lighted cigar in one hand and two fingers of the other upraised in his habitual V-sign.

'Good old Winnie!' cheered the immediate crowds and when his car was swallowed by the crowds ahead agreed in amicable bellows that the old geezer didn't look like he was short of a drop and why not seeing he'd done a proper job and might've been a different turn-up for the book had he not been on the job – no telling, mind – still, credit where credit was due – Good old Winnie! Good old you! Good old me! Good old us!

It was eight o'clock before they found footholds, and Charles a handhold, on the Victoria Memorial, high enough for them to see over the ocean of heads the cause of the latest ecstatic cheers. A policeman had lost his helmet. Another outburst, when it was returned to him by the crowd, and then some of the policeman's answer was passed back and up the Victoria Memorial. 'Reckons not much less than the half-million just along of here and up The Mall. Never seen no crowds to beat today's in his life, that cop hasn't.'

The youngish civilian on Charles's right who was supporting his wife, or girlfriend, announced that it didn't surprise him neither seeing it just taken them nigh on the three hours from Notting Hill Gate. 'Stopped for a drop, mind, and drop it was! Least half-pints the landlord had in the house,' he added ruefully, then all four laughed as if he had made the joke of the century.

Sarah, leaning against Charles and holding his enfolding arm to keep her balance, looked in amazement over the

177

human ocean and wondered why it did not frighten her even although she knew it was just one of the oceans now over-flowing Central London and the embankments on both sides of the Thames. She too had never seen, or even imagined the possibility of, crowds of these sizes; but all that she had seen, and was seeing now, were good-humoured, uproariously cheerful, with very rare exceptions, sober, and continuously, euphorically, bemoaning the last. . . . Ruddy typical, that's what, mate! Government's forgotten to order the beer! . . . What say, mate? Not heard beer's gone on ration and not got your beer coupons? . . . That's right, lady – you wants to get along the Town Hall for your beer coupons – pull the other one? . . . Would I tell a lie? And me, sober as a judge – fetch me black cap – someone's swinging for this but seeing there's no room to swing a cat – let's have a bit of a song. . . .

Sarah thought suddenly, I know exactly why I'm not frightened. How could I be? I've nursed them for years – met them for years – met, known, liked, admired, and, at times, loved them. So has Charles, in the wards, in Cas., in the Army – for years and years and that's why, though he turned into a clam for most of the Prof.'s party, ever since we hit the crowds he's been chatting to strangers as if they were his old buddies. And that's how they're all chattering to us. Is that something Charles and I owe Martha's? No, I don't think so. At least, not just Martha's, as I don't think in peacetime we could have got as close to the patients – to people – as in war. The war made us realise we were all in it together, and once the British realise that, they merge into one, and merge into friends. Like now. So no one is frightening or frightened, as who wants to frighten or be frightened by an old friend? When enjoying themselves with friends, who gives a damn about elbows in ribs, accidentally knocked-off glasses, or crushed toes? Any more for the Skylark? . . . Move along down the car, please? . . . Room for a small one . . . shift up, mate . . .

in you come, missus . . . makes a nice change, don't it, lady? . . . can't rightly credit there'll be no more bombs, rockets and them nasty doodlebugs. . . .

Dear God, thought Sarah, how they hated the doodles and so did I – far more than the old bombs, far more than the rockets – and oh, the relief of knowing all that really is over – and that's it! Yes, I know I'm right! What is fundamentally powering all this is relief. Not triumph. Just plain relief and the gratitude that follows that relief. The gratitude at having survived and of being able to see that despite the years of battering and burning so much of London has survived. The gratitude to those that didn't survive and paid for today with their lives, whether in the services or civvy street. Because if the civvies hadn't taken it and had caved in, we wouldn't now be shouting our heads off – Good old you – me – us – as we all know that those that didn't make it to today were US. . . .

Charles, feeling the new tension in her small, soft body, hitched her higher to ask anxiously in her ear, 'What's up?'

She looked into his concerned face. 'Just relief-syndrome hitting.'

He understood immediately. 'Lot of it about, Sarah. Hell of a lot of it about.'

'Just thinking that.' She kissed his thin cheek, then protested smilingly, 'Slacken the half-Nelson, chum! I'm an odd type. Need to breathe.'

'Sorry.' He smiled shyly and lowered her to her former position, then, a few minutes later hitched her up again and in the cover of 'Here they come!' from roughly half-a-million throats, demanded in a different tone, 'Why aren't you singing "There'll Always Be An England"?'

Her eyes laughed. 'And have my Scottish paternal grandmother turn in her grave?'

'You've never told me you've Scots blood!'

'You've never told me I'm different and that's what you like about me!'

179

He yelped with laughter and had to kiss her before reluctantly lowering her and turning his attention to the figures now on the balcony of Buckingham Palace. In the evening light the figures looked very small and as they waved and smiled gave Charles the immediate impression that they were astounded and moved by the size of the crowd and the audible note of affection now lacing the crescendo of cheering. King George and Princess Elizabeth were in Army khaki, Queen Elizabeth wore blue, the school-age Princess Margaret Rose, pink, and the ubiquitous Mr Churchill, black jacket and pin-striped. For once he was cigarless, which evoked wild cheers.

The balcony was empty when Charles and Sarah, supported and balanced by other hands, climbed down from the Victoria Memorial. They left its occupants still observing to each other that while some Royals over the Channel scarpered soon as Jerry poked in his nose, Our Guv' and his Good Lady stuck it out in London same as us. And they had the one through their own roof so it was no use saying that when an HE (high explosive bomb), a landmine, a doodlebug or a rocket got your moniker on it it made any difference if what you got on your bonce was a titfer or a crown.

It was growing dark before they reached Birdcage Walk. 'Charles, we'll have to re-think. We'll never make the river in time for the lights.'

'We will. Get behind me, grab my respirator strap with one hand, give me the other and hang on tight.' He grasped her right hand and by using his height, powerful shoulders, free left hand to tap on other shoulders and disgraceful, unashamed cheating, began edging them through the crowd. 'Excuse me, sir – madam – old chap – so sorry to shove but I'm a Medical Officer, my girlfriend's a nurse and we've got to get back to St Martha's Hospital – yes, on-duty – thanks so much – excuse me, sir. . . .'

Sarah, clinging on, followed him breathlessly, admiringly and unashamedly, through Birdcage Walk, Parliament Square and onto the first few yards of the right-hand pavement of Westminster Bridge where they were stopped by the police.

'Sorry, sir. No more on the bridge. Don't want to fetch it down now Jerry's packed in that job, do we?'

'Point taken, officer. All right if we stay here?'

'Here, but not the one step more, sir.' It was now very dark and the policeman's shadowy outline was as tall but much bulkier than Charles's. 'You and your young lady struck it lucky, sir. Front stalls and no standing room left either side the river.'

'Dead lucky,' agreed Charles, feeling Sarah gently kicking his right leg. He glanced back and upwards at the towering black shadow of Big Ben. 'Not long to go.'

'Just a few minutes, sir.' The policeman moved away.

Charles slid Sarah in front of him and into the front rank on their bit of pavement. She leant against him to look up at his shadowed face. 'You've just shaken me rigid! You did a marvellous job getting us here, but I've never even suspected that you could play dirty.'

He smiled hugely in the darkness. 'Even Homer sometimes nods and, as could be said, on some counts you don't know me all that well.' He looked over the surrounding heads. 'I must get you back up. You should see what I'm seeing.'

A few seconds later Sarah's arm was across his shoulders and, with their faces level, they looked together over what appeared to be a thick, uneven black carpet spangled with millions of jerkily dancing glowworms that sprawled over embankments, main and side streets, monuments, statues and flattened bombsites, divided only by the river running like black oil. The glowworms were the tips of lighted cigarettes in millions of invisible heads and the carpet was made of massed invisible heads . From the carpet came the growling roaring of millions of expectant voices, and the roaring rose and fell like the waves of a great, happy, confluence of oceans.

Sarah caught her breath. 'Must be more than a million here?'

'I'd say probably around two. Could be wrong. Comfortable?'

'Fine, but how about you? You've been toting me on and off, for hours.'

'No complaints.' Suddenly, he breathed in sharply. 'Hold everything,' he whispered instinctively.

Suddenly, the massed glowworms were stilled, the masses of voices silenced and Big Ben had begun chiming half-past ten on the night of 8th May, 1945. And then, before the chimes died away, suddenly, over the bridges, along both embankments, in all the visible main and side streets and in what seemed to be every building, the lights came on together. And if not every street lamp bulb was working and every blackout screen and brick knocked out, after nearly six years of darkness it looked as if the entire great, sprawling, burnt, battered, bruised and indomitable city blazed with light.

At the impact of that light, for two or three seconds that recalled to Sarah and innumerable others, the seconds between a rocket's flash and explosion, the silence was unbroken. It was as if none dared trust reality and feared it a mirage that would vanish as swiftly as it had appeared. Then, slowly, almost hesitantly, the cheering returned and rose to previously unheard heights. Not merely great waves, but tidal wave after tidal wave, rolling on and on over millions of heads, on and on over standing buildings, roofless buildings, jagged walls, flattened bombsites, unfilled craters; over the river, down the river and over the docks; up river and over the devastated City that so many of those now cheering had seen burn in the great fire raids at the dying end of 1940. By tonight it had only one-third of its peacetime buildings standing, but still had gloriously and gently visible the dome of St Paul's.

It was common knowledge that London had not yet sufficient power for the lights to remain on all tonight, but the thought of the return of darkness for no more serious reason than a lack of electricity only gilded the ecstasy. Chances were (and to be proved) THEY'd scrape up enough power to get the lights back on for another spell tomorrow night, but who was bothered about tomorrow when tonight – TONIGHT – you'd just watched the lights come back on!

Charles saw the tears pouring down Sarah's face and, on looking around, noticed every woman in his sight was weeping and so were many men. He was conscious that his own eyes smarted and of his own verbal inadequacy when most moved. 'Worth seeing,' he murmured.

Sarah dried her face. 'One day, maybe, we'll tell our grandchildren we saw the lights of London come on again.' She gave a long shuddering sigh. 'I just hope to God they'll never be able to understand why we made such a song and dance about it.'

There was so much he longed to say, but being, amongst all else, a realist, he said all he could say just then, 'I hope to God you're right, Sarah.'

AUGUST, 1945

CHAPTER ELEVEN

'YOU'LL be wanting King's Road end of Beaufort Street for that number, miss,' called the taximan over his shoulder.

Sarah didn't hear. She was alone in the back of a taxi temporarily stopped by traffic in the inside westbound lane crossing Westminster Bridge, and her concentration was held by a group of American soldiers being lectured by a guide at the exact spot from where she and Charles had watched the lights come on three months and two days ago, in their last meeting. All the GIs were strung with cameras, and had their backs to Westminster and eager attention fixed on the south bank at which the guide was gesticulating. He was a small man whose greasy black hat, long black overocat and trailing, grubby white scarf made him a living prototype of Sid Field's mythical spiv 'Slasher Green from the Elephant and Castle' and his stentorian voice floated through the open taxi window ' . . . and it was down along of there, gents – I tell you no lies – it was down along of there as Jack the Ripper wrought his fell deeds. . . . '

The taximan, having checked in his driving mirror, glanced indulgently at the cause of his fare's inattention and shouted back more loudly, 'Wouldn't mind having a bob for every Yank that's been told the tale of Jack the Ripper since old Jerry packed it in and old Ike been fetching 'em over on leaf in their hordes. More Yanks in London now than you could shake a stick at, miss, but not saying they're not welcome nor had the bit of leaf coming. Wouldn't like to say what might not have happened if they'd not come over to lend the hand, miss.'

Sarah roused herself from thoughts far removed from Jack the Ripper, but not from GIs, and, still watching them, thought aloud. 'Nor me – but they all look so young.'

'Would be, wouldn't they, miss? What I means is, not having been in as long as our lot they've not had to use all from Boy Soldiers to the old Pioneer Corps.' The traffic was still stopped, so he took a longer look in his driving mirror. Nice little bit of fluff back there – on the pale side, mind, and a good bit of kip wouldn't come amiss neither – but didn't look more than an half-pint slip of a girl in that pretty little blue cotton summer dress. It looked like it seen a few washes in its time but had been washed and ironed nice for the holidays he reckoned she was off on from the old leather suitcase he'd just fetched into the back for her. 'Just starting up old Martha's, are you, miss? What they calls a pro?'

Sarah smiled. 'Thanks. No. I'm a staff nurse – ' his hand moved to the clock 'hold it, driver, please! This one's on me. I've spent chunks of the war free-riding in London taxis and I'm terribly grateful to you all but I'm not going on-duty now. And anyway – ' she glanced at her still unread evening paper on the back seat and her eyes and voice grew guarded 'could be all over.'

'I'll not say you're wrong there, miss, but I don't like – '

'I know and thanks a lot. Do me a favour?'   –

'If you insists, miss, much obliged.' He returned his hand to the wheel and as the traffic began moving it was a few minutes before he shouted, 'What you reckon to these atomic bombs, miss?'

'I don't know, driver. I just don't know.'

'Makes you think,' he said and then drove the rest of the way in silence.

It was nearly eight o'clock on the evening of Friday, 10th August, 1945, and last Tuesday, 7th August, *The Times* and other British newspapers and the BBC news had briefly announced that sixteen hours earlier a solitary US aircraft had dropped one atomic bomb on Hiroshima, the seventh largest town in Japan, that was situated at the entrance to an inland sea of several tributaries of the river Ota, and possessed a large harbour, factories, oil refineries and large military garrison in addition to its civilian population. Most of those first reports had explained that 'Hiroshima' in English translation was 'the broad island', but carried little about the size of the bomb or what an atomic explosion involved. But to a war-orientated, much-bombed country, the fact that only one bomb and bombing aircraft had been used immediately announced that the Allies now possessed a new and dreadful weapon and that it was – just possible – that its use might end the Far East war without General MacArthur's now daily expected Armed Invasion of Japan. He was reputed to estimate that such an invasion must cause his Forces approximately one million casualties and, inevitably, even greater Japanese military and civilian losses, to which, as inevitably, must be added the lives of all the Allied prisoners-of-war in Japan's custody.

On the following day, Wednesday, 8th August, those first impressions were underlined by the news that Russia had belatedly declared war upon Japan and invaded Manchuria. All the rest of that day, as all the previous days, in public and in private, hopes of Japan's speedy unconditional surrender had been high, and unfulfilled. Then, today, had come the news that yesterday, Thursday, 9th August, another single US aircraft had dropped another single atomic bomb on the port of the Japanese city of Nagasaki. Once again, the first reports on the second bomb to reach the British public had been as brief as those on the first, but by now there was far greater coverage of what had happened to Hiroshima after the bomb dropped last Monday.

Sarah first heard Tuesday's news from Paddy Brown when he swept into Alex for the first morning round and uncharacteristically forgot to exchange his usual smiles and waves with the patients. For once, none of the patients noticed, being either too ill, too newly post-operative, or too engrossed in listening to their wireless headphones that, as ever, were not switched on until after morning prayers. Paddy was alone and temporarily acting-SMO as Dr Roberts was one of the last victims of the summer flu that during June and July had so decimated the staff that Sarah's long overdue final week of last year's three weeks' annual holiday had been postponed from early June to the end of the second week in August. It was not only the flu — from which Sarah escaped — that had stretched the staff in the last two months; Val and nearly all their set had had to leave to start Government-ordained midwifery or TB nursing courses. Sarah had been granted one year's reservation from starting National Service, signed a one-year contract for the official post of Alex's staff nurse and had her salary raised to sixty pounds a year. She still wore her old fourth-year uniform, as material for new staff nurses' dresses was not yet available. And on Tuesday she was in charge as Sister Alex had been granted the special day off to attend her younger sister's wedding.

Paddy, his long white coat flapping around his long narrow figure, ostensibly studied the open log book and murmured, 'Seen a paper yet?'

She looked sharply at his lowered black head. He knew Alex's papers arrived mid-morning and that she didn't own a wireless. Her mind shot to Charles in Germany, then across the world. 'MacArthur invaded?' she queried without moving her lips.

He glanced up sombrely. 'Not like you mean. Kicked-off with a V3.'

190

Her eyes widened. 'We've got one?'

'Lay a year's pay.' He repeated what he had just read in *The Times*.

She was incredulous. 'Just – one – ?'

'Just the one.' He straightened as they looked at each other in the same way, and then his quick dark gaze ranged up and down the long, tidy, still window-bricked and artifically lighted ward. 'Had pal Jerry had this little number up his sleeve, you'd now be twanging your harp, I'd be toasting, and the lovely Val would be looking right where she belongs instead of learning to deliver sprogs to appease Ernie Bevin and – who knows? – maybe even catching on to the odd fact of life, which just goes to show that even our new masters may have the odd good point even if you'd not find me laying good money on it.'

She ignored most of those remarks. She was far too disturbed to be bothered about his lovelife or another of his tirades on the Labour Party's sweeping victory in last month's first General Election for ten years and the havoc that, in his conviction, Mr Aneurin Bevan was bound to cause the entire British medical profession. 'What exactly is an atomic bomb?'

'Mother of God, girl, how would I know? I'm no damned scientist! Just a damned physician – so let's get stuck in.' He hitched on his most charming smile like a mask and sauntered to the medical side. 'And a very good morning to you, ladies. . . . '

After Paddy's round and before the arrival of the surgeons, Sarah put her head round the kitchen door. 'Do me a favour, Daisy. Catch the newspaper boy and get me a *Times* and dump it in the flat bathroom.' She handed over threepence. 'I'm bound to be tied-up when he shows up.'

'I dunno, nurse. If it's not the one thing it's the other,' retorted Daisy, taking the money and referring equally to the very heavy ward, new staff of student nurses, Sister Alex's private grief on her sister's wedding day and the

191

latest war-gen she had just collected when returning the breakfast trolley to the main kitchen. Then, having literally changed her tunes from the end of the European war, she spent all her kitchenbased morning singing softly 'Pistol packin' Moma' in place of 'Don't Fence Me In'.

Val Martin's leaving date in late June had been shortly followed by Nurse Grey's move to the basement theatre, Nurse Burton's to Casualty, and the return of Nurse Yates's set to the Hut. This so pleased Nurse Yates secretly that the vehemence of her protests at being chucked back to the sticks only just fell short of those of every Martha's man but Charles with whom Sarah had discussed Mr Bevan's plans for a future National Health Service. These discussions in Martha's, London, were incessant and invariably ended 'if Nye Bevan's allowed to get away with it we'll all be reduced to Slave-labour.' Charles's only comment upon it in his letters to Sarah had been, 'Like you, I'm for it.'

Alex's new senior student nurse, although a senior third-year, was not yet an SRN, and at one-thirty an Office Sister relieved Sarah for late lunch and her two-to-five. After the handing-over report, Sarah went into the flat bathroom, closed the door and sat on the edge of the empty bath to read her waiting newspaper. She had read the account she sought twice, when the door opened.

'Really, Nurse Thane!' The Office Sister was in the doorway. 'One would not expect to have to remind a staff nurse temporarily acting-Sister that St Martha's nurses do not loll around their wards reading gossip columns!'

'Sorry, Sister.' Sarah leapt up, outwardly polite and inwardly seething. No wonder we win our ruddy wars — haven't the imagination to do anything else, she fumed mentally, storming out of the flat and into a posse of new-up-from-the-Hut-last-evening's dressers streaking from Casualty to the nearest basement stairs to the staff canteen. 'Sorry,' she muttered as they scattered, and from her cursory glance she didn't recognise any.

'Hi, Nurse Thane. Long time, no see.'

She looked up in surprise at the tall, very thin young man that had broken from the others to address her, and had to draw on her training to control her expression. 'Hi, Mr Hastings. Sorry, miles away,' she added truthfully, though that was not why she had failed to recognise him. He seemed to her to have shed a couple of stones, gained about ten years and have only his height in common with the excited, schoolboyish figure preening himself in new battledress at their last meeting. She looked around. The others had gone. 'Where's your chum Mr Dunlop?'

'Still tied-up in the SSO's morning clinic in Cas.' He stiffened as if anticipating a blow – or a question – and glared over her head at a bricked window. 'Why are all our bloody bricks still in situ, nurse?'

She eyed him empathetically and took the cue. 'Because the Ministry of Works or Whatever responsible for getting on with the job of shifting them, hasn't. According to the grapevine Matron and our pundits have been narking non-stop in high places, but presumably, Messrs Attlee, Bevan and Co. have other things on their minds.'

'Good God, nurse, don't bring up that so-and-so Nye Bevan! Do you realise that if he's allowed to get away with it we'll all be – ' suddenly, his voice stopped.

'Clean round the bend,' she put in quickly and thought, no, you can't voice 'slave-labour' as you, too, know, and I don't think will ever be able to forget, what the reality of that term looked like. She went on without pause, 'If the old firm's anything to go on, Mr Bevan's already got the British medical profession two-thirds round. This joint's been rocked by mutinous medical groans and those wretched bricks haven't helped, especially in Cas. in the heat we've had lately. The sandbags may've gone, but Dacey says even Sister Cas. is getting so narked at still being shut in behind blast walls and bricked windows that he doesn't think she'd be at all sorry if some of you dressers

193

got busy with pickaxes whilst she's off-duty.'

He brightened a little. 'No kidding, nurse?' She shook her head. 'Think Dacey could scrounge us pickaxes?'

She smiled. 'Mr Hastings, Dacey can scrounge anyone anything, anytime. But get your timing right. Even if Sister Cas. is off, don't risk it between nine and six weekdays, as patients are always in and out and the Cas. staff'll have to stop you. Pick a quiet early evening — like Friday — no one wants to be sick pay-day evening if it can possibly be postponed — hold it!' She thought a moment. 'Yes, Sister Cas. is off this coming weekend.'

'Good show.' There was more than the ghost of his former self in his grin. 'Thanks, nurse. Jolly decent running into you again. Nurse Burton tipped me off this morning that you're still in Alex, but she said you'd gone to glory. Where's the snappy grey dress, long sleeves, cuffs and all that?'

'Like the bricks, someone hasn't come up with the necessary yet.'

'Tough show. But, congrats and all that.'

'Thanks.' She hesitated, then she said, 'And to you and your lot for all this and that.'

His grin and youth vanished from his face. 'You — er — read — of course.'

'Bit more than that. A friend of mine was in one of the first RAMC units in and, aside from a twenty-four over here, stayed put till our flame-throwers burnt it to the ground in — late May, wasn't it?'

He nodded tensely. 'Martha's man?'

'C.R. Bradley.'

'Tall, fair chap? Yep. Saw him.' He stared at the floor. 'Yep Saw him,' he repeated mechanically and, glancing up, noticed the paper under his arm. 'Know something, nurse? They were saying over the water that Jerry was close as hell to his V_3.'

'Why not? He'd already thought up the doodles and

rockets.' They looked at each other as she and Paddy had earlier. 'Better get weaving, Mr Hastings, or your chums'll finish the new biscuits. Tuesday. New rations. Remember?'

He was still far away. 'Why in hell is it always Tuesday?' he demanded and strode off before she could answer. She looked after him thoughtfully and then grimaced painfully at her thoughts. She had walked nearly to the dining-room when a new thought exploded in her mind – if one bomb dropped five miles above target can blitz a town, who will ever dare start another world war?

The absolute novelty in that thought so mentally stunned Sarah that she drifted through lunch, went back to the Home, climbed out of her window and leant upon the roof's parapet in as near a state of trance as it was possible for her to be whilst retaining physiological control of her senses. Eventually the trance released its grip sufficiently for her to recognise its presence, and she thought slowly – I've never felt like this before, but how could I? Never before have I lived in a world that's suddenly become so dangerous and – yes! – and so much safer! Or is that contradiction crazy? I don't know. I just don't know. . . .

It was some time later, when she was gazing down at the uncleared ruins of the hospital, that another explosive thought, but this time a purely personal and, at face value, totally irrational one hit her – I want to go home. But she understood immediately what her mind was telling her, and was turning this over carefully, lovingly, like an unexpected precious gift that needed to be unwrapped and examined from all sides with great delicacy, when Nurse Mayhew, back on day-duty and the new owner of Val's old room, pushed up her window to call, 'Phone, Nurse Thane! Nurse Martin!'

Val was on her weekly day off from the Maternity Unit that was forty miles from London and fifteen from her home. 'I'm ringing from home. Daddy said I could. He's in

195

such a tiz about this atomic bomb – he says once people start splitting atoms they'll probably blow up the world so why worry about phone bills – as I wanted to catch you and guessed you'd be two-to-five as isn't this Sister's wedding day – you know what I mean.'

'Yes, to the lot and how – '

'Oh, poor Sister! Awful for her. I don't know how she can face it, I couldn't, but I expect she will – but this isn't why I'm ringing. I thought you'd like to know I had an awfully nice letter from Charles last week thanking me for mine.'

Sarah was intrigued. 'I didn't know you'd written to him.'

'I forgot to tell you when we last nattered. But – well – you know poor John's name was in the casualty lists three weeks ago – '

'Yes. I wrote you.'

'So you did. Sorry. Forgot. Anyway, I'd never had the chance to thank Charles for saving me months of – you know – so I wrote to him care of Martha's and he got it in a few days, he says and, actually, he seemed pleased about it.'

'I'm sure he was.' Sarah's mind had gone into fast-motion. 'What did you say?'

'Oh, just that I was – you – well – you've had to write that sort of letter and really it only needs half a page but as he'd taken so much trouble explaining about poor darling John I had to fill mine out a bit so I told him about midder and your flu epidemic postponing your holiday. Didn't he tell you?'

'No. I expect he forgot,' lied Sarah.

'He says he's pretty busy. But this isn't only why I'm ringing. What are you doing about your holiday? Mummy and Daddy have asked me to tell you that if you aren't fixed up they'd love to have you spend the week here.'

Up to a minute back Sarah had made no plans for the holiday she had intentionally not mentioned to Charles to avoid upsetting him, especially, on her behalf. She suddenly felt as if she had just had a glass of champagne, and said truthfully, 'Val, that's terribly kind of your parents and please thank them very much, but an old family friend has laid things on for me.'

'Oh, goody! I've been fearfully worried about your having nowhere to go.'

And, being kind-hearted, told Charles, thought Sarah. And he went quietly into action – and I've only just seen it. My God, am I dumb and is that man crafty! Crafty and damned lovable. She thanked Val for her concern and switched subjects. 'How's midder?'

'Non-stop hectic. I've never worked so hard in my life and Sarah – never – have a baby! The babies are perfect poppets but having babies is so – so messy! No – it's all very well for you to laugh – but, honestly, I just don't know how the mums face it! I'll just never be able to face it – and how's Alex?'

Sarah, translating correctly, said the medical side was still packed with post-flu chest complications and Paddy had forgotten what time off was.

'Poor Paddy. His postcard said he was acting, unpaid SMO and it shouldn't happen to a Chinaman. I don't know why a Chinaman, but it made me laugh. He always does, though I often don't understand his jokes – but he really is rather sweet even though, as I always said, he's nothing really like my poor darling John. Did I tell you I had a perfectly sweet letter from his mother?'

'No. But I'm glad for her and you.'

'She said something like that and that when the war's all over and the Government here released civvy-trained nurses she and her husband would love to meet me, and why don't I take a long holiday with them in Kenya and perhaps nurse out there. Mummy and Daddy aren't too keen on this, but, actually, I think I'd rather like it. What do you think?'

'That it's a marvellous idea and you should keep it open. Your parents probably need time to get used to it, and they should have time as, even if the war ends, tomorrow, it'll take months, if not longer, before enough trained nurses are demobbed from the Services to ease the situation in civvy hospitals and let us off the hook.'

They talked for a few more minutes. After they had rung off, Sarah went back to her room and opened the drawer that contained all Charles's letters and the smallish, registered packet she had had from his solicitors last week and a couple of days after his last letter. In that packet were Charles's spare keys to his flat and a letter that began 'Further to the instructions of our client Captain C. R. Bradley, MC, RAMC, we enclose herewith. . . . ' -

She took out Charles's last letter that at first reading had struck her as unusually thought-provoking. Re-reading it now, it hit her like a second glass of champagne.

You asked if you could do anything about the Beaufort Street flat. Now, yes please and here's why; Mrs Rawton, the owner, wants to sell and has offered me first refusal at what my solicitors say is a fair price. I'm thinking of taking this up. A London base could be handy and will certainly be rare as snowflakes in hell when this show's finally over, and here again, I'm dead lucky for this offer. But I would very much like you to take a look at the joint and give me your views before I decide. No sweat here. Tenancy's mine till end of this September. (Yes, I know, bit of wasted cash, but could prove worth it.)

Mrs R. being v. helpful and since I left has arranged for her former cleaner to go in weekly and been in herself a few times and with my written okay shifted out the articles she doesn't want included in the deal – i.e. furniture, fittings and lease with 84 years to go – fair enough, wouldn't you say?

I hope you won't mind my jumping the gun, but I've written to my solicitors – London firm that handled my uncle's affairs till he died in '40 and then took over mine – asking them to send you my spare keys, as you'll be keeping an eye on the place for me and I hope using it occasionally as it does property no good to stand empty. I've let Mrs R know this too. So if you care to use it for the odd weekend off, or at any time you want a bit of a break, you'll do it good. But, of course, if you'd rather not be involved, forget it, shove the keys in a drawer and let me have them back when I get back.

I can't say when this'll be. Having recently had leave – yes, I know, sick-leave, but to the Army leave is leave – and, in any event, I'm a non-com. and rightly the coms. [combatants] have first pick. As for the job here – in comparison, cleaning up the Augean Stables was a piece of cake. Incidentally, did you know the Germans were convinced penicillin was just a bit of our propaganda? No longer, so we're roughly having to keep the stuff under armed guard as its local black market price has hit the sky.

That's enough for tonight.

Except, as you know, I love and miss you like hell. Take care, please.

Goodnight.

Charles.

Sarah put away the letter and again went out onto the roof and leant on the parapet and looked down at the uncleared ruins and the unremoved huge notices, ST MARTHA'S HOSPITAL. DOWN BUT NOT OUT. OPEN TO ALL PATIENTS and PLEASE HELP OUR RE-BUILDING FUND above the old, wooden, padlocked collecting boxes. 'Please help,' she thought, oh yes. He had spotted that from Val's letter, and got cracking. He knows I've no home to go to, can't afford an hotel, loathe the idea of scrounging on friends, and would spend my holiday in

199

this Home if he hadn't set this up so tactfully that I've only just caught on, but if I hadn't, or didn't want to, I could shoot it down without having to feel guilty. I'm not shooting it down, but I've got to be dead crafty. One breath of it on the grapevine would hurt his Martha's future as much as mine. A world war may be at its last gasp; the world may have changed since yesterday; but Martha's won't change and nor, yet, have the absurd conventional attitudes that will automatically take his giving me the freedom of his flat as proof that we've been to bed together. Prof. Pathology could look the other way were I not a Martha's nurse, but as I am, he couldn't. So I won't even put this on paper to Charles. I'll tell him what I think of his flat, but not how I intend using it, till he gets back – but it's a marvellous idea, as a break right away is just what I need. I am so tired, she thought, staring down at the old blast walls, and if only for a week – I do so want to go home.

'Four bob it says on the clock, miss. Four bob is what I takes.' The taximan politely returned Sarah's tip. 'Much obliged. Just step down and give you a hand in with that case.'

'I can manage, thanks. Ground floor. And thank you very much.'

'A pleasure, miss. All the best.'

'And to you.'

She waved him off, picked up the case and turned to look at the cracked, chipped, smoke- and grime-blackened exterior of the house in the tall row of semi-terraced Victorian conversions where Charles had one of the two ground-floor flats. The communal wooden front door was high, narrow, half-open; its peeling paintwork was so filthy it was impossible to guess its real colour, but since this, as the condition of the building's exterior, was so similar to others all over London, Sarah's only immediate impressions were that the structure must be as strong as it looked to have survived so much, and also very lucky. She was particularly grateful for the last; the past was still far too present for her to ignore the part luck plays in all lives. A minute later she had unlocked and closed behind her the front door of Charles's empty flat with such a strong sensation of having done this often that she had consciously to remind herself this was not merely for the first time but breaking a habit strictly instilled in her from early girlhood. Her reaction to that reminder was a quick, and not wholly self-derisive, grin.

The front door opened into a narrow, longish passage that on her near left ended at the open front room door, and at the other end, from Charles's earlier verbal descriptions, in the single large bedroom beyond which lay a smaller one that the owner had used as a boxroom and that he thought would make a rather decent little study, or something, as it had a good window overlooking the minute back garden that went with the flat. Despite being buried in weeds and debris, the garden had distinct possibilities, he'd thought. The bathroom and kitchen lay between the two ends and off the other side of the passage. The hall had several long cracks in its faded, duck-blue painted walls, and a long, narrow, worn navy carpet, but the paintwork was clean and carpet well brushed.

She left her case in the passage and went first into the front room, absently taking with her the paper she had bought whilst waiting to flag down a taxi outside the Home. Knowing Dacey's acumen, she had not risked asking him to get her a taxi and had intentionally left the Home a few minutes after Home Sister left for Sisters' supper in the hospital dining-room. Being a staff nurse, Sarah was no longer officially required to leave more than a forwarding address with her authorities, and owing to her well-timed departure she had been able to leave a brief message for Home Sister with the Home's portress,

201

explaining no forwarding address was necessary as she intended staying in London and would be back regularly for her post.

The large, squarish front room was a little chilly, as it faced north, but it was as clean as the passage and had an attractive bay window and its own quota of cracks in walls and ceiling. But the faded cream and tan colour scheme was pleasant, the old leather sofa and its matching armchairs on either side of the empty, open hearth, looked comfortable, and, like the two empty mahogany bookcases and one lowish table, had an Edwardian solidity. Nothing short of a direct hit would have destroyed this lot, thought Sarah, switching on the light and rejoicing in being able to leave open the long, faded, tan valvet curtains heavily lined with blackout material. I'll take this for granted one day, she thought smiling at herself, but that day hasn't come yet.

She dropped her sling bag and paper in the armchair facing the window, intending to continue her tour. Then she changed her mind and sat down to enjoy for a few more minutes the lights coming on in the houses across the road, the pale glow of the street lights in the lingering twilight, the room's associations with Charles that for her were so strong and so welcome that she had to remind herself of the trap of wishful thinking, and the sheer wonder of being free to sit and stare and think her own thoughts. She kicked off her shoes and relaxed, gratefully, in the chair that was as comfortable as it looked. And as she had just ended her twelfth working day since her last weekend off, it was about a minute before she was asleep. In another fifteen minutes Charles's taxi from Charing Cross drew up outside and, having already seen his front room lights, he leapt out, and glimpsing her small sleeping figure through the uncurtained window, he handed the driver a pound note and told him to keep the change.

It was another twelve hours before Sarah woke to find that it was daylight, all the electric lights were off, and that she was lying outstretched and face down on the sofa, loosely covered by a clean sheet and a couple of blankets, with her right cheek pressed into the clean linen case of a soft pillow, and could smell coffee and cigarette smoke. She was immediately wide awake, so before she twisted herself around she knew what she would see; that knowledge so overwhelmed her with happiness that for a few moments it left her speechless. All she could do was lie back and smile at Charles sitting upon one arm of the chair in which she had fallen asleep and in which he had later spent the night with his feet on the opposite chair. He'd not wanted to risk waking her by carrying her along to the bedroom, or risk her suddenly waking alone in strange surroundings. He had bathed and shaved and had on a clean uniform shirt and tie and his service dress trousers, and was sipping coffee, and smoking, and watching her with his customary quietness, and at the back of his eyes even more wonder than when he had watched the lights of London come on again.

Sarah looked from him to the two armchairs drawn closer together than when she had fallen asleep, to the small tray on the table that was set with a white china coffee pot, clean cup and saucer and a small plate of Naafi biscuits. 'If you insist,' she said almost casually, 'I'll answer to Goldilocks.'

He smiled slowly and very wonderfully. 'I don't. In any event, you weren't sleeping in my bed.'

'Nor were you.' She raised herself and leant against the sofa arm and pushed her short dark hair from her face that more than long sleep had so transformed that she looked touchingly young and genuinely beautiful.

Charles rose carefully but even so spilt some of his coffee when he put the cup onto its waiting saucer. 'Black without, okay? Sorry, no milk. Haven't yet been out to see what I can scrounge.'

'Do fine, thanks.' As she expected, he handed her the coffee without touching her, and their eyes continued the unspoken conversation that had begun when she woke and smiled at him. 'When did you get here?'

'Approx. 1900.'

'Oh – Charles – I'm sorry.'

He backed to the empty hearth and, kicking the chairs aside, stood with his hands in his trouser pockets. 'Why?'

'Well – just wish I'd known.'

'You couldn't. Didn't know myself till yesterday morning. I'd been trying to twist arms and pull strings since Val slipped me the gen you've kept under cover – '

'But you knew why – '

'Of course. Anyway, all I could previously have hoped for was a forty-eight sometime in this next week, and then yesterday morning – ' he paused to glance at her evening paper that was still on the floor. 'They said seven days, and if you step on it, the RAF'll have you in Gatwick this evening.' He looked back at her. 'I stepped on it and came straight here intending then to ring your Home as I didn't think your holiday started until Friday. Finding I was wrong made – er – rather a nice homecoming.'

She suddenly felt too weak to do more than mutter, 'Seven – whole – days?'

He nodded, knowing she was trying to accept the situation that it had taken him several hours of last night to accept. He lit two cigarettes together then went over to hand her one and stayed standing by her. It was a good minute before Sarah could speak and then only in a whisper. 'God Almighty. It must be all over.'

'Yes,' he said calmly, whilst his eyes caressed her. 'If MacArthur doesn't have the Jap surrender today, he will in the next few days. After these two bombs, Japan knows it's had it. So, just possibly, Prof. Path. may have one son back. Not a hope in hell of that if MacArthur had had to invade. The Japs had no need of POW hostages as they don't hold with their chaps being taken prisoner and would sure as hell have bumped off their Allied lot as soon as the first enemy landing craft hit their beaches.'

'I've been thinking on those lines since this Tuesday.' Her mind flashed back to the GIs on the bridge last evening. 'I've been thinking, I just don't know, about these bombs. They sound so terrible.'

'They are. Each one, thousand plus, casualties.'

'But if MacArthur had had to invade – millions?' He inclined his head. 'So, since Tuesday, I've gone in circles, not knowing what I thought. Only now – ' she hesitated and looked up at him gravely 'now, at least I do know exactly what I'd think if I were the wife, mother, sister, girlfriend, of anyone in MacArthur's Invasion Force, as I've been there too. Three times.' His suddenly altered expression seemed nearly to stop her heart, but she kept on. 'I'd thank God for anything that stopped this war, because if that anything was – is – dreadful enough to stop this one it must – it just must – stop another world war from starting up just as soon as another generation's old enough to tote guns – as happened to ours.' Again, she hesitated. Then, 'Charles, am I crazy? Or do you think – honestly think – that after spending all our lives either in the shadow of, or actually in, a war our lot might now have the luck to – to get old?'

He said slowly, 'I don't think you're crazy, Sarah. I was working on this last night. I think you're right.' A small, and still incredulous smile flickered over his strong, plain, good-humoured face. 'We – and I don't just mean you and I – could have a future.' He glanced around the room as if seeing it for the first time. 'So knocked me for six, that one, that if you hadn't been kipping a couple of yards off to account for my pulse-rate, I'd have taken my own temp.' He looked down into her face. 'Thinking of those grandchildren you once mentioned didn't exactly lower the rate. Mind telling me now, was that – er – a purely academic observation?'

She looked straight up into his passionately tender,

loving, questioning eyes, and was honest. 'I think, probably, it was mostly academic on VE night, Charles, though obviously – ' she blushed faintly 'it was a Freudian slip.'

'I – er – did wonder about that.' His deep voice was a little unsteady. 'It wasn't something I cared to bring up in letters. Needs a good morning light. Like – now. So how do you feel now about our telling them our tales of this and that?'

She had to drag away her gaze to rest it briefly upon the two chairs in which he had spent the night.

She looked back at him and waved at the chairs. 'We'll probably have to bribe them with sweets, and their parents'll nark like crazy at our spoiling them, but I'm now sure it's a good idea.' She held out both hands. 'Okay?'

'Couldn't be better,' said Charles, suddenly lifting her off the sofa. 'I kid you not, my dearest Sarah – couldn't be bloody better.'

THE END

MY FRIEND THE PROFESSOR

by Lucilla Andrews

Frances Dorland was coping with all the physical and emotional problems of a young probationer nurse when she first met her friend, the professor. A gentle, quiet man, he was to prove a loyal and undemanding friend throughout the pressures and demands of her training life.

It was not until her dearest friend, Estelle, was fighting for her life on the dangerously ill list, that she discovered the truth about Mr Slane, her friend the professor.

0552 08719   £1.75

A HOSPITAL SUMMER

by Lucilla Andrews

SUMMER 1940 – AN ENGLISH MILITARY HOSPITAL – AND A YOUNG NURSE FACES THE REALITIES OF DUNKIRK AND THE BATTLE OF BRITAIN.

Few novels have captured the wartime atmosphere of a military hospital as effectively as *A Hospital Summer*. The twenty-year-old Clare Dillon, almost overnight, learns the harsh realities of love and war.

'It has bite, shrewdness and even toughness in it, and in spite of dealing with life and death, as they were encountered by a VAD, it manages to be continually humorous'

Lawrence Meynell, *Express and Star*

0552 085412   £1.75

A SELECTED LIST OF FINE NOVELS
AVAILABLE FROM CORGI BOOKS

THE PRICES SHOWN BELOW WERE CORRECT AT THE TIME OF GOING TO PRESS. HOWEVER TRANSWORLD PUBLISHERS RESERVE THE RIGHT TO SHOW NEW RETAIL PRICES ON COVERS WHICH MAY DIFFER FROM THOSE PREVIOUSLY ADVERTISED IN THE TEXT OR ELSEWHERE.

☐ 08541 3	A HOSPITAL SUMMER	*Lucilla Andrews*	£1.75
☐ 08719 X	MY FRIEND THE PROFESSOR	*Lucilla Andrews*	£1.75
☐ 09505 2	HOSPITAL CIRCLES	*Lucilla Andrews*	£1.75
☐ 12638 1	SPINNERS WHARF	*Iris Gower*	£2.95
☐ 12637 3	PROUD MARY	*Iris Gower*	£2.95
☐ 12387 0	COPPER KINGDOM	*Iris Gower*	£2.50
☐ 12565 2	LAST YEAR'S NIGHTINGALE	*Claire Lorrimer*	£2.95
☐ 10584 8	MAVREEN	*Claire Lorrimer*	£2.95
☐ 11207 0	TAMARISK	*Claire Lorrimer*	£2.95
☐ 11726 9	CHANTAL	*Claire Lorrimer*	£2.95
☐ 12182 7	THE WILDERLING	*Claire Lorrimer*	£2.95
☐ 11959 8	THE CHATELAINE	*Claire Lorrimer*	£2.95
☐ 12607 1	DOCTOR ROSE	*Elvi Rhodes*	£1.95
☐ 11596 7	FEET IN CHAINS	*Kate Roberts*	£1.95
☐ 11685 8	THE LIVING SLEEP	*Kate Roberts*	£2.50
☐ 12579 2	THE DAFFODILS OF NEWENT	*Susan Sallis*	£1.75
☐ 12375 7	A SCATTERING OF DAISIES	*Susan Sallis*	£2.50

All these books are available at your book shop or newsagent, or can be ordered direct from the publisher. Just tick the titles you want and fill in the form below.

TRANSWORLD PUBLISHERS, Cash Sales Department,
61-63 Uxbridge Road, Ealing, London W5 5SA

Please send a cheque or postal order, not cash. All cheques and postal orders must be in £ sterling and made payable to Transworld Publishers Ltd.

Please allow cost of book(s) plus the following for postage and packing:

UK/Republic of Ireland Customers: Orders in excess of £5; no charge. Orders under £5; add 50p

Overseas Customers: All orders; add £1.50

NAME (Block Letters)..

ADDRESS ....

....

Lucilla Andrews was born in Suez, the second daughter of an English father and a Spanish mother. Her late father was then a manager in the Eastern Telegraph Company. At three she began her education in an English private girls' boarding school in Sussex and when she was eleven she wrote her first novel – an epic of love, lust and banditry in China. Unfortunately, the manuscript was discovered and ended up in the school incinerator.

During World War II, Lucilla Andrews entered the Nightingale Training School at St. Thomas's Hospital in London and five years later left with an S.R.N. and S.C.M. Part One. She married a doctor, had one child, and when her husband's illness necessitated that she become the family breadwinner, she returned to nursing.

Her first book, *The Print Petticoat*, was written while she was working as an assistant Night Sister in a small Sussex hospital. Since that time it has never been out of print.

Over the years Lucilla Andrews has established herself as one of Britain's leading popular novelists. She created what was virtually a new genre – the hospital romance – written against an authentic and detailed medical background drawn from her own experience.

Readers who would like to know more about Lucilla Andrews are recommended to read her autobiography, *No Time For Romance*, an account of her life and training as a nurse in wartime London.

Lucilla Andrews lives in Edinburgh

Also by Lucilla Andrews

A HOSPITAL SUMMER
MY FRIEND THE PROFESSOR
HOSPITAL CIRCLES

and published by Corgi Books

THE LIGHTS
OF LONDON

Lucilla Andrews

CORGI BOOKS

THE LIGHTS OF LONDON

A CORGI BOOK   0 552 12756 6

Originally published in Great Britain by William Heinemann Ltd.

PRINTING HISTORY
William Heinemann edition published 1985
Corgi edition published 1987

This book is set in 10 on 11pt Garamond

Corgi Books are published by Transworld Publishers Ltd.,
61-63 Uxbridge Road, Ealing, London W5 5SA, in Australia by
Transworld Publishers (Australia) Pty. Ltd., 15-23 Helles Avenue,
Moorebank, NSW 2170, and in New Zealand by Transworld
Publishers (N.Z.) Ltd., Cnr. Moselle and Waipareira Avenues,
Henderson, Auckland.

Printed and bound in Great Britain by
Cox & Wyman Ltd, Reading